Paul Leicester Ford

The Great Train Robbery

Paul Leicester Ford

The Great Train Robbery

ISBN/EAN: 9783743372702

Manufactured in Europe, USA, Canada, Australia, Japa

Cover: Foto ©Andreas Hilbeck / pixelio.de

Manufactured and distributed by brebook publishing software (www.brebook.com)

Paul Leicester Ford

The Great Train Robbery

The Great K. & A. Train-Robbery

By

Paul Leicester Ford

Author of The Honorable Peter Stirling

New York

Dodd Mead and Company

1897

Contents

CONTENTS

THE
Great K. & A. Train-Robbery

CHAPTER I

THE PARTY ON SPECIAL NO. 218

ANY one who hopes to find in what is here written a work of literature had better lay it aside unread. At Yale I should have got the sack in rhetoric and English composition, let alone other studies, had it not been for the fact that I played half-back on the team, and so the professors marked me away up above where I ought to have ranked. That was twelve years ago, but my life since I received my parchment has hardly been of a kind to improve me in either style or grammar. It is true that one woman tells me I write well, and my directors never find fault with my compositions; but I know that she likes my letters because, whatever else they may say to her, they always say in some form, "I love you," while my board approve my annual reports because thus far I have been able to end each with "I recommend the declaration of a dividend of— per cent from the earnings of the current year." I should therefore prefer to reserve my writings for such friendly critics, if it did not seem necessary to make public a plain statement concerning an affair over which there appears to be much confusion. I have heard in the last five years not less than twenty renderings of what is commonly called "the great K. & A. train-robbery," — some so twisted and distorted that but for the intermediate versions I should never have recognized them as attempts to narrate the series of events in which I played a somewhat prominent part. I have read or been told that, unassisted, the pseudo-hero captured a dozen desperadoes; that he was one of the road agents himself; that he was saved from lynching only by the timely arrival of cavalry; that the action of the

United States government in rescuing him from the civil authorities was a most high-handed interference with State rights; that he received his reward from a grateful railroad by being promoted; that a lovely woman as recompense for his villany — but bother! it's my business to tell what really occurred, and not what the world chooses to invent. And if any man thinks he would have done otherwise in my position, I can only say that he is a better or a worse man than Dick Gordon.

Primarily, it was football which shaped my end. Owing to my skill in the game, I took a post-graduate at the Sheffield Scientific School, that the team might have my services for an extra two years. That led to my knowing a little about mechanical engineering, and when I left the " quad " for good I went into the Alton Railroad shops. It was n't long before I was foreman of a section; next I became a division superintendent, and after I had stuck to that for a time I was appointed superintendent of the Kansas & Arizona Railroad, a line extending from Trinidad in Kansas to The Needles in Arizona, tapping the Missouri Western System at the first place, and the Great Southern at the other. With both lines we had important traffic agreements, as well as the closest relations, which sometimes were a little difficult, as the two roads were anything but friendly, and we had directors of each on the K. & A. board, in which they fought like cats. Indeed, it could only be a question of time when one would oust the other and then absorb my road. My head-quarters were at Albuquerque, in New Mexico, and it was there, in October, 1890, that I received the communication which was the beginning of all that followed.

This initial factor was a letter from the president of the Missouri Western, telling me that their first vice-president, Mr. Cullen (who was also a director of my road), was coming out to attend the annual election of the K. & A., which under our charter had to be held in Ash Forks, Arizona. A second paragraph told me that Mr. Cullen's family accompanied him, and that they all wished to visit the Grand Cañon of the Colorado on their way. Finally the president wrote that the party travelled in his own private car, and asked me to make myself generally useful to them. Having become quite hardened to just such demands, at the proper date I ordered my superintendent's car on to No. 2, and the next morning it was dropped off at Trinidad.

The moment No. 3 arrived, I climbed into the president's special, that was the last car on the train, and introduced myself to Mr. Cullen, whom, though an official of my road, I had never met. He seemed surprised at my presence, but greeted me very pleasantly as soon as I explained that the Missouri Western office had asked me to do what I could for him, and that I was there for that purpose. His party were about to sit down to breakfast, and he asked me to join them: so we passed into the dining-room at the forward end of the car, where I was introduced to " My son," " Lord Ralles," and

" Captain Ackland." The son was a junior copy of his father, tall and fine-looking, but, in place of the frank and easy manner of his sire, he was so very English that most people would have sworn falsely as to his native land. Lord Ralles was a little, well-built chap, not half so English as Albert Cullen, quick in manner and thought, being in this the opposite of his brother Captain Ackland, who was heavy enough to rock-ballast a road-bed. Both brothers gave me the impression of being gentlemen, and both were decidedly good-looking.

After the introductions, Mr. Cullen said we would not wait, and his remark called my attention to the fact that there was one more place at the table than there were people assembled. I had barely noted this, when my host said, " Here's the truant," and, turning, I faced a lady who had just entered. Mr. Cullen said, " Madge, let me introduce Mr. Gordon to you." My bow was made to a girl of about twenty, with light brown hair, the bluest of eyes, a fresh skin, and a fine figure, dressed so nattily as to be to me, after my four years of Western life, a sight for tired eyes. She greeted me pleasantly, made a neat little apology for having kept us waiting, and then we all sat down.

It was a very jolly breakfast-table, Mr. Cullen and his son being capital talkers, and Lord Ralles a good third, while Miss Cullen was quick and clever enough to match the three. Before the meal was over I came to the conclusion that Lord Ralles was in love with Miss Cullen, for he kept making low asides to her; and from the fact that she allowed them, and indeed responded, I drew the conclusion that he was a lucky beggar, feeling, I confess, a little pang that a title was going to win such a nice American girl.

One of the first subjects spoken of was train-robbery, and Miss Cullen, like most Easterners, seemed to take a great interest in it, and had any quantity of questions to ask me.

" I 've left all my jewelry behind, except

my watch," she said, "and that I hide every night. So I really hope we'll be held up, it would be such an adventure."

"There isn't any chance of it, Miss Cullen," I told her; "and if we were, you probably wouldn't even know that it was happening, but would sleep right through it."

"Wouldn't they try to get our money and our watches?" she demanded.

I told her no, and explained that the ex-press- and mail-cars were the only ones to which the road agents paid any attention. She wanted to know the way it was done: so I described to her how sometimes the train was flagged by a danger signal, and when it had slowed down the runner found himself covered by armed men; or how a gang would board the train, one by one, at way stations, and then, when the time came, steal forward, secure the express agent and postal clerk, climb over the tender, and com-pel the runner to stop the train at some lonely spot on the road. She made me tell

her all the details of such robberies as I
knew about, and, though I had never been
concerned in any, I was able to describe
several, which, as they were monotonously
alike, I confess I colored up a bit here and
there, in an attempt to make them interest-
ing to her. I seemed to succeed, for she
kept the subject going even after we had left
the table and were smoking our cigars in
the observation saloon. Lord Ralles had a
lot to say about the American lack of courage
in letting trains containing twenty and thirty
men be held up by half a dozen robbers.

"Why," he ejaculated, " my brother and
I each have a double express with us, and do
you think we'd sit still in our seats? No.
Hang me if we would n't pot something."

"You might," I laughed, a little nettled,
I confess, by his speech, " but I'm afraid it
would be yourselves."

"Aw, you fancy resistance impossible?"
drawled Albert Cullen.

"It has been tried," I answered, "and
without success. You can see it's like all

surprises. One side is prepared before the other side knows there is danger. Without regard to relative numbers, the odds are all in favor of the road agents."

"But I would n't sit still, whatever the odds," asserted his lordship. "And no Englishman would."

"Well, Lord Ralles," I said, "I hope for your sake, then, that you 'll never be in a hold-up, for I should feel about you as the runner of a locomotive did when the old lady asked him if it was n't very painful to him to run over people. 'Yes, madam,' he sadly replied: 'there is nothing musses an engine up so.'"

I don't think Miss Cullen liked Lord Ralles's comments on American courage any better than I did, for she said, —

"Can't you take Lord Ralles and Captain Ackland into the service of the K. & A., Mr. Gordon, as a special guard?"

"The K. & A. has never had a robbery yet, Miss Cullen," I replied, "and I don't think that it ever will have."

" Why not ? " she asked.

I explained to her how the Cañon of the Colorado to the north, and the distance of the Mexican border to the south, made escape so almost desperate that the road agents preferred to devote their attentions to other routes. " If we were boarded, Miss Cullen," I said, " your jewelry would be as safe as it is in Chicago, for the robbers would only clean out the express- and mail-cars; but if they should so far forget their manners as to take your trinkets, I'd agree to return them to you inside of one week."

" That makes it all the jollier," she cried, eagerly. " We could have the fun of the adventure, and yet not lose anything. Can't you arrange for it, Mr. Gordon ? "

" I'd like to please you, Miss Cullen," I said, "and I'd like to give Lord Ralles a chance to show us how to handle those gentry; but it's not to be done." I really should have been glad to have the road agents pay us a call.

We spent that day pulling up the Raton

pass, and so on over the Glorietta pass down to Lamy, where, as the party wanted to see Santa Fé, I had our two cars dropped off the overland, and we ran up the branch line to the old Mexican city. It was well-worn ground to me, but I enjoyed showing the sights to Miss Cullen, for by that time I had come to the conclusion that I had never met a sweeter or jollier girl. Her beauty, too, was of a kind that kept growing on one, and before I had known her twenty-four hours, without quite being in love with her, I was beginning to hate Lord Ralles, which was about the same thing, I suppose. Every hour convinced me that the two understood each other, not merely from the little asides and confidences they kept exchanging, but even more so from the way Miss Cullen would take his lordship down occasionally. Yet, like a fool, the more I saw to confirm my first diagnosis, the more I found myself dwelling on the dimples at the corners of Miss Cullen's mouth, the bewitching uplift of her upper lip, the runaway curls about her neck, and the curves and color of her cheeks.

Half a day served to see everything in Santa Fé worth looking at, but Mr. Cullen decided to spend there the time they had to wait for his other son to join the party. To pass the hours, I hunted up some ponies, and we spent three days in long rides up the old Santa Fé trail and to the outlying mountains. Only one incident was other than pleasant, and that was my fault. As we were riding back to our cars on the second afternoon, we had to cross the branch road-bed, where a gang happened to be at work tamping the ties.

" Since you're interested in road agents, Miss Cullen," I said, " you may like to see one. That fellow standing in the ditch is Jack Drute, who was concerned in the D. & R. G. hold-up three years ago."

Miss Cullen looked where I pointed, and seeing a man with a gun, gave a startled jump, and pulled up her pony, evidently supposing that we were about to be attacked.

" Sha'n't we run ? " she began, but then checked herself, as she took in the facts of the drab clothes of the gang and the two armed men in uniform. " They are con- victs ? " she asked, and when I nodded, she said, " Poor things ! " After a pause, she asked, " How long is he in prison for ? "

" Twenty years," I told her."

" How harsh that seems ! " she said. " How cruel we are to people for a few moments' wrong-doing, which the circum- stances may almost have justified ! " She checked her pony as we came opposite Drute, and said, " Can you use money ? "

" Can I, lyedy ? " said the fellow, leering in an attempt to look amiable. " Wish I had the chance to try."

The guard interrupted by tel...ng her it was n't permitted to speak to the convicts while out of bounds, and so we had to ride on. All Miss Cullen was able to do was to throw him a little bunch of flowers she had gathered in the mountains. It was literally casting pearls before swine, for the fellow did not seem particularly pleased, and when, late that night, I walked down there with a lantern I found the flowers lying in the ditch. The experience seemed to sadden and distress Miss Cullen very much for the rest of the afternoon, and I kicked myself for having called her attention to the brute, and could have knocked him down for the way he had looked at her. It is curious that I felt thankful at the time that Drute was not holding up a train Miss Cullen was on. It is always the unexpected that happens. If I could have looked into the future, what a strange variation on this thought I should have seen!

The three days went all too quickly, thanks to Miss Cullen, and by the end of that time I began to understand what love really meant to a chap, and how men could come to kill each other for it. For a fairly sensible, hard-headed fellow it was pretty quick work, I acknowledge; but let any man have seven years of Western life without seeing a woman worth speaking of, and

then meet Miss Cullen, and if he did n't do
as I did, I would n't trust him on the tail-
board of a locomotive, for I should put him
down as defective both in eyesight and in
intellect.

CHAPTER II

THE HOLDING-UP OF OVERLAND NO. 3

On the third day a despatch came from Frederic Cullen telling his father he would join us at Lamy on No. 3 that evening. I at once ordered 97 and 218 coupled to the connecting train, and in an hour we were back on the main line. While waiting for the overland to arrive, Mr. Cullen asked me to do something which, as it later proved to have considerable bearing on the events of that night, is worth mentioning, trivial as it seems. When I had first joined the party, I had given orders for 97 to be kicked in between the main string and their special, so as not to deprive the occupants of 218 of the view from their observation saloon and balcony platform. Mr. Cullen came to me now and asked me to reverse the arrangement and make my car the tail end. I was giving orders for the splitting and kicking in when No. 3 arrived, and thus did not see the greeting of Frederic Cullen and his family. When I joined them, his father told me that the high altitude had knocked his son up so, that he had to be helped from the ordinary sleeper to the special and had gone to bed immediately. Out West we have to know something of medicine, and my car had its chest of drugs: so I took some tablets and went into his state-room. Frederic was like his brother in appearance, though not in manner, having a quick, alert way. He was breathing with such difficulty that I was almost tempted to give him nitroglycerin, instead of strychnine, but he said he would be all right as soon as he became accustomed to the rarefied air, quite pooh-poohing my suggestion that he take No. 2 back to Trinidad; and while I was still urging, the train started. Leaving him the vials of digitalis and strychnine, therefore, I went back, and dined *solus* on my own car, indulging at the end in a cigar, the smoke of which would keep turning into pictures of Miss Cullen. I have thought about those pictures since then, and have concluded that when cigar-smoke behaves like that, a man might as well read his destiny in it, for it can mean only one thing.

After enjoying the combination, I went to No. 218 to have a look at the son, and found that the heart tonics had benefited him considerably. On leaving him, I went to the dining-room, where the rest of the party were still at dinner, to ask that the invalid have a strong cup of coffee, and after delivering my request Mr. Cullen asked me to join them in a cigar. This I did gladly, for a cigar and Miss Cullen's society were even pleasanter than a cigar and Miss Cullen's pictures, because the pictures never quite did her justice, and, besides, did n't talk.

Our smoke finished, we went back to the saloon, where the gentlemen sat down to poker, which Lord Ralles had just learned, and liked. They did not ask me to take a hand, for which I was grateful, as the salary of a railroad superintendent would hardly stand the game they probably played; and I had my compensation when Miss Cullen also was not asked to join them. She said she was going to watch the moonlight on the mountains from the platform, and opened the door to go out, finding for the first time that No. 97 was the " ender." In her disappointment she protested against this, and wanted to know the why and wherefore.

" We shall have far less motion, Madge," Mr. Cullen explained, " and then we sha'n't have the rear-end man in our car at night."

" But I don't mind the motion," urged Miss Cullen, " and the flagman is only there after we are all in our rooms. Please leave us the view."

" I prefer the present arrangement, Madge," insisted Mr. Cullen, in a very positive voice.

I was so sorry for Miss Cullen's disappointment that on impulse I said, " The platform of 97 is entirely at your service, Miss Cullen." The moment it was out I realized that I ought not to have said it, and that I deserved a rebuke for supposing she would use my car.

Miss Cullen took it better than I hoped for, and was declining the offer as kindly as my intention had been in making it, when, much to my astonishment, her father interrupted by saying, —

" By all means, Madge. That relieves us of the discomfort of being the last car, and yet lets you have the scenery and moonlight."

Miss Cullen looked at her father for a moment as if not believing what she had heard. Lord Ralles scowled and opened his mouth to say something, but checked himself, and only flung his discard down as if he hated the cards.

" Thank you, papa," responded Miss Cullen, " but I think I will watch you play."

" Now, Madge, don't be foolish," said Mr. Cullen, irritably. " You might just as well have the pleasure, and you 'll only disturb the game if you stay here."

Miss Cullen leaned over and whispered

something, and her father answered her. Lord Ralles must have heard, for he muttered something, which made Miss Cullen color up; but much good it did him, for she turned to me and said, " Since my father doesn't disapprove, I will gladly accept your hospitality, Mr. Gordon," and after a glance at Lord Ralles that had a challenging " I 'll do as I please " in it, she went to get her hat and coat. The whole incident had not taken ten seconds, yet it puzzled me beyond measure, even while my heart beat with an unreasonable hope; for my better sense told me that it simply meant that Lord Ralles disapproved, and Miss Cullen, like any girl of spirit, was giving him notice that he was not yet privileged to control her actions. Whatever the scene meant, his lordship did not like it, for he swore at his luck the moment Miss Cullen had left the room.

When Miss Cullen returned we went back to the rear platform of 97. I let down the traps, closed the gates, got a camp-stool for her to sit upon, with a cushion to lean back on, and a footstool, and fixed her as comfortably as I could, even getting a travelling-rug to cover her lap, for the plateau air was chilly. Then I hesitated a moment, for I had the feeling that she had not thoroughly approved of the thing and therefore she might not like to have me stay. Yet she was so charming in the moonlight, and the little balcony the platform made was such a tempting spot to linger on, while she was there, that it was n't easy to go. Finally I asked, —

" You are quite comfortable, Miss Cullen ?"

" Sinfully so," she laughed.

" Then perhaps you would like to be left to enjoy the moonlight and your meditations by yourself ? " I questioned. I knew I ought to have just gone away, but I simply could n't when she looked so enticing.

" Do you want to go ? " she asked.

" No ! " I ejaculated, so forcibly that she gave a little startled jump in her chair. " That is — I mean," I stuttered, embarrassed by my own vehemence, "I rather thought you might not want me to stay."

"What made you think that?" she demanded.

I never was a good hand at inventing explanations, and after a moment's seeking for some reason, I plumped out, "Because I feared you might not think it proper to use my car, and I suppose it's my presence that made you think it."

She took my stupid fumble very nicely, laughing merrily while saying, "If you like mountains and moonlight, Mr. Gordon, and don't mind the lack of a chaperon, get a stool for yourself, too." What was more, she offered me half of the lap-robe when I was seated beside her.

I think she was pleased by my offer to go away, for she talked very pleasantly, and far more intimately than she had ever done before, telling me facts about her family, her Chicago life, her travels, and even her thoughts. From this I learned that her elder brother was an Oxford graduate, and that Lord Ralles and his brother were classmates, who were visiting him for the first time since

he had graduated. She asked me some questions about my work, which led me to tell
her pretty much everything about myself that
I thought could be of the least interest; and
it was a very pleasant surprise to me to find
that she knew one of the old team, and had
even heard of me from him.

"Why," she exclaimed, "how absurd of
me not to have thought of it before! But,
you see, Mr. Colston always speaks of you
by your first name. You ought to hear how
he praises you."

"Trust Harry to praise any one," I said.
"There were some pretty low fellows on the
old team, — men who could n't keep their
word or their tempers, and would slug every
chance they got; but Harry used to insist
there was n't a bad egg among the lot."

"Don't you find it very lonely to live out
here, away from all your old friends?" she
asked.

I had to acknowledge that it was, and told
her the worst part was the absence of pleasant women. "Till you arrived, Miss Cul-

len," I said, " I had n't seen a well-gowned woman in four years." I 've always noticed that a woman would rather have a man notice and praise her frock than her beauty, and Miss Cullen was apparently no exception, for I could see the remark pleased her.

" Don't Western women ever get Eastern gowns ? " she asked.

" Any quantity," I said, "but you know, Miss Cullen, that it is n't the gown, but the way it 's worn, that gives the artistic touch." For a fellow who had devoted the last seven years of his life to grades and fuel and rebates and pay-rolls, I don't think that was bad. At least it made Miss Cullen's mouth dimple at the corners.

The whole evening was so eminently satisfactory that I almost believe I should be talking yet, if interruption had not come. The first premonition of it was Miss Cullen's giving a little shiver, which made me ask if she was cold.

" Not at all," she replied. " I only — what place are we stopping at ? "

I started to rise, but she checked the movement and said, "Don't trouble yourself. I thought you would know without moving. I really don't care to know."

I took out my watch, and was startled to find it was twenty minutes past twelve. I was n't so green as to tell Miss Cullen so, and merely said, "By the time, this must be Sanders."

"Do we stop long?" she asked.

"Only to take water," I told her, and then went on with what I had been speaking about when she shivered. But as I talked it slowly dawned on me that we had been standing still some time, and presently I stopped speaking and glanced off, expecting to recognize something, only to see alkali plain on both sides. A little surprised, I looked down, to find no siding. Rising hastily, I looked out forward. I could see moving figures on each side of the train, but that meant nothing, as the train's crew, and, for that matter, passengers, are very apt to alight at every stop. What did mean something was that there was no water-tank, no station, nor any other visible cause for a stop.

"Is anything the matter?" asked Miss Cullen.

"I think something's wrong with the engine or the road-bed, Miss Cullen," I said, " and, if you'll excuse me a moment, I'll go forward and see."

I had barely spoken when "bang! bang!" went two shots. That they were both fired from an English "express" my ears told me, for no other people in this world make a mountain howitzer and call it a rifle.

Hardly were the two shots fired when "crack! crack! crack! crack!" went some Winchesters.

"Oh! what is it?" cried Miss Cullen.

"I think your wish has been granted," I answered hurriedly. "We are being held up, and Lord Ralles is showing us how to—"

My speech was interrupted. "Bang! bang!" challenged another "express," the shots so close together as to be almost simultaneous. " Crack ! crack ! crack ! " retorted the Winchesters, and from the fact that silence followed I drew a clear inference. I said to myself, " That is an end of poor John Bull."

CHAPTER III

A NIGHT'S WORK ON THE ALKALI PLAINS

I HURRIED Miss Cullen into the car, and, after bolting the rear door, took down my Winchester from its rack.

"I'm going forward," I told her, "and will tell my darkies to bolt the front door: so you'll be as safe in here as in Chicago."

In another minute I was on my front platform. Dropping down between the two cars, I crept along beside — indeed, half under — Mr. Cullen's special. After my previous conclusion, my surprise can be judged when at the farther end I found the two Britishers and Albert Cullen, standing there in the most exposed position possible. I joined them, muttering to myself something about Providence and fools.

"Aw," drawled Cullen, "here's Mr. Gordon, just too late for the sport, by Jove."

"Well," bragged Lord Ralles, "we've had a hand in this deal, Mr. Superintendent, and have n't been potted. The scoundrels broke for cover the moment we opened fire."

By this time there were twenty passengers about our group, all of them asking questions at once, making it difficult to learn just what had happened; but, so far as I could piece the answers together, the poker-players' curiosity had been aroused by the long stop, and, looking out, they had seen a single man with a rifle, standing by the engine. Instantly arming themselves, Lord Ralles let fly both barrels at him, and in turn was the target for the first four shots I had heard. The shooting had brought the rest of the robbers tumbling off the cars, and the captain and Cullen had fired the rest of the shots at them as they scattered. I did n't stop to hear more, but went forward to see what the road agents had got away with.

I found the express agent tied hand and

foot in the corner of his car, and, telling a brakeman who had followed me to set him at liberty, I turned my attention to the safe. That the diversion had not come a moment too soon was shown by the dynamite cartridge already in place, and by the fuse that lay on the floor, as if dropped suddenly. But the safe was intact.

Passing into the mail-car, I found the clerk tied to a post, with a mail-sack pulled over his head, and the utmost confusion among the pouches and sorting-compartments, while scattered over the floor were a great many letters. Setting him at liberty, I asked him if he could tell whether mail had been taken, and, after a glance at the confusion, he said he could not know till he had examined.

Having taken stock of the harm done, I began asking questions. Just after we had left Sanders, two masked men had entered the mail-car, and while one covered the clerk with a revolver the other had tied and "sacked" him. Two more had gone forward and done the same to the express agent. Another had climbed over the tender and ordered the runner to hold up. All this was regular programme, as I had explained to Miss Cullen, but here had been a variation which I had never heard of being done, and of which I could n't fathom the object. When the train had been stopped, the man on the tender had ordered the fireman to dump his fire, and now it was lying in the road-bed and threatening to burn through the ties; so my first order was to extinguish it, and my second was to start a new fire and get up steam as quickly as possible. From all I could learn, there were eight men concerned in the attempt; and I confess I shook my head in puzzlement why that number should have allowed themselves to be scared off so easily.

My wonderment grew when I called on the conductor for his tickets. These showed nothing but two from Albuquerque, one from Laguna, and four from Coolidge. This latter would have looked hopeful but for the fact that it was a party of three women and a man. Going back beyond Lamy did n't give anything, for the conductor was able to account for every fare as either still in the train or as having got off at some point. My only conclusion was that the robbers had sneaked onto the platforms at Sanders; and I gave the crew a good dressing down for their carelessness. Of course they insisted it was impossible; but they were bound to do that.

Going back to 97, I got my telegraph instrument, though I thought it a waste of time, the road agents being always careful to break the lines. I told a brakeman to climb the pole and cut a wire. While be was struggling up, Miss Cullen joined me.

" Do you really expect to catch them ? " she asked.

" I should n't like to be one of them," I replied.

" But how can you do it ? "

" You could understand better, Miss Cullen, if you knew this country. You see every bit of water is in use by ranches, and those fellows can't go more than fifty miles without watering. So we shall have word of them, wherever they go."

" Line cut, Mr. Gordon," came from overhead at this point, making Miss Cullen jump with surprise.

" What was that ? " she asked.

I explained to her, and, after making connections, I called Sanders. Much to my surprise, the agent responded. I was so astonished that for a moment I could not believe the fact.

" This is the queerest hold-up of which I ever heard," I remarked to Miss Cullen.

" Aw, in what respect ? " asked Albert Cullen's voice, and, looking up, I found that he and quite a number of the passengers had joined us.

" The road agents make us dump our fire," I said, " and yet they have n't cut the wires in either direction. I can't see how they can escape us."

" What fun ! " cried Miss Cullen.

" I don't see what difference either makes in their chance of escaping," said Lord Ralles.

While he was speaking, I ticked off the news of our being held up, and asked the agent if there had been any men about Sanders, or if he had seen any one board the train there. His answer was positive that no one could have done so, and that settled it as to Sanders. I asked the same questions of Allantown and Wingate, which were the only places we had stopped at after leaving Coolidge, getting the same answers. That eight men could have remained concealed on any of the platforms from that point was impossible, and I began to suspect magic. Then I called Coolidge, and told of the holding up, after which I telegraphed the agent at Navajo Springs to notify the commander at Fort Defiance, for I suspected the road agents would make for the Navajo reservation. Finally I called Flagstaff as I had Coolidge, directed that the authorities be notified of the facts, and ordered an extra to bring out the sheriff and posse.

"I don't think," said Miss Cullen, "that I am a bit more curious than most people, but it has nearly made me frantic to have you tick away on that little machine and hear it tick back, and not understand a word."

After that I had to tell her what I had said and learned.

"How clever of you to think of counting the tickets and finding out where people got on and off! I never should have thought of either," she said.

"It hasn't helped me much," I laughed, rather grimly, "except to eliminate every possible clue."

"They probably did steal on at one of the stops," suggested a passenger.

I shook my head. "There isn't a stick of timber nor a place of concealment on these alkali plains," I replied, "and it was bright moonlight till an hour ago. It would be hard enough for one man to get within a mile of the station without being seen, and it would be impossible for seven or eight."

" How do you know the number ? " asked a passenger.

" I don't," I said. " That's the number the crew think there were; but I myself don't believe it."

" Why don't you believe the men ? " asked Miss Cullen.

" First, because there is always a tendency to magnify, and next, because the road agents ran away so quickly."

" I counted at least seven," asserted Lord Ralles.

" Well, Lord Ralles," I said, " I don't want to dispute your eyesight, but if they had been that strong they would never have bolted, and if you want to lay a bottle of wine, I'll wager that when I catch those chaps we'll find there weren't more than three or four of them."

" Done ! " he snapped.

Leaving the group, I went forward to get the report of the mail agent. He had put things to rights, and told me that, though the mail had been pretty badly mixed up, only one pouch at worst had been rifled. This — the one for registered mail — had been cut open, but, as if to increase the mystery, the letters had been scattered, unopened, about the car, only three out of the whole being missing, and those very probably had fallen into the pigeon-holes and would be found on a more careful search.

I confess I breathed easier to think that the road agents had got away with not...ng, and was so pleased that I went back to the wire to send the news of it, that the fact might be included in the press despatches. The moon had set, and it was so dark that I had some difficulty in finding the pole. When I found it, Miss Cullen was still standing there. What was more, a man was close beside her, and as I came up I heard her say, indignantly, —

" I will not allow it. It is unfair to take such advantage of me. Take your arm away, or I shall call for help "

That was enough for me. One step carried my hundred and sixty pounds over the intervening ground, and, using the momentum of the stride to help, I put the flat of my hand against the shoulder of the man and gave him a shove. There are three or four Harvard men who can tell what that means, and they were braced for it, which this fellow was n't. He went staggering back as if struck by a cow-catcher, and lay down on the ground a good fifteen feet away. His having his arm around Miss Cullen's waist unsteadied her so that she would have fallen too if I had n't put my hand against her shoulder. I longed to put it about her, but by this time I did n't want to please myself, but to do only what I thought she would wish, and so restrained myself.

Before I had time to finish an apology to Miss Cullen the fellow was up on his feet, and came at me with an exclamation of anger. In my surprise at recognizing the voice as that of Lord Ralles, I almost neglected to take care of myself; but, though he was quick with his fists, I caught him by the wrists as he closed, and he had no chance after that against a fellow of my weight.

" Oh, don't quarrel ! " cried Miss Cullen.

Holding him, I said, " Lord Ralles, I overheard what Miss Cullen was saying, and, supposing some man was insulting her, I acted as I did." Then I let go of him, and, turning, I continued, " I am very sorry, Miss Cullen, if I did anything the circumstances did not warrant," while cursing myself for my precipitancy and for not thinking that Miss Cullen would never have been caught in such a plight with a man unless she had been half willing; for a girl does not merely threaten to call for help if she really wants aid.

Lord Ralles was n't much mollified by my explanation. " You 're too much in a hurry, my man," he growled, speaking to me as if I were a servant. " Be a bit more careful in the future."

I think I should have retorted — for his manner was enough to make a saint mad — if Miss Cullen had n't spoken.

" You tried to help me, Mr. Gordon, and I am deeply grateful for that," she said. The words look simple enough set down here. But the tone in which she said them, and the extended hand and the grateful little squeeze she gave my fingers, all seemed to express so much that I was more puzzled over them than I was over the robbery.

CHAPTER IV

SOME RATHER QUEER ROAD AGENTS

" You had better come back to the car, Miss Cullen," remarked Lord Ralles, after a pause.

But she declined to do so, saying she wanted to know what I was going to telegraph; and he left us, for which I was n't sorry. I told her of the good news I had to send, and she wanted to know if now we would try to catch the road agents. I set her mind at rest on that score.

" I think they 'll give us very little trouble to bag," I added, " for they are so green that it 's almost pitiful."

" In not cutting the wires ? " she asked.

" In everything," I replied. " But the worst botch is their waiting till we had just passed the Arizona line. If they had held us up an hour earlier, it would only have been State's prison."

" And what will it be now ? "

" Hanging."

" What ? " cried Miss Cullen.

" In New Mexico train-robbing is not capital, but in Arizona it is," I told her.

" And if you catch them they 'll be hung ? " she asked.

" Yes."

" That seems very hard."

The first signs of dawn were beginning to show by this time, and as the sky brightened I told Miss Cullen that I was going to look for the trail of the fugitives. She said she would walk with me, if not in the way, and my assurance was very positive on that point. And here I want to remark that it 's saying a good deal if a girl can be up all night in such excitement and still look fresh and pretty, and that she did.

I ordered the crew to look about, and then began a big circle around the train. Finding nothing, I swung a bigger one. That being equally unavailing, I did a larger third. Not a trace of foot or hoof within a half-mile of the cars! I had heard of blankets laid down to conceal a trail, of swathed feet, even of leathern horse-boots with cattle-hoofs on the bottom, but none of these could have been used for such a distance, let alone the entire absence of any signs of a place where the horses had been hobbled. Returning to the train, the report of the men was the same.

"We've ghost road agents to deal with, Miss Cullen," I laughed. "They come from nowhere, bullets touch them not, their lead hurts nobody, they take nothing, and they disappear without touching the ground."

"How curious it is!" she exclaimed. "One would almost suppose it a dream."

"Hold on," I said. "We do have something tangible, for if they disappeared they left their shells behind them." And I pointed to some cartridge-shells that lay on the ground beside the mail-car. "My theory of aerial bullets won't do."

"The shells are as hollow as I feel," laughed Miss Cullen.

"Your suggestion reminds me that I am desperately hungry," I said. "Suppose we go back and end the famine."

Most of the passengers had long since returned to their seats or berths, and Mr. Cullen's party had apparently done the same, for 218 showed no signs of life. One of my darkies was awake, and he broiled a steak and made us some coffee in no time, and just as they were ready Albert Cullen appeared, so we made a very jolly little breakfast. He told me at length the part he and the Britishers had borne, and only made me marvel the more that any one of them was alive, for apparently they had jumped off the car without the slightest precaution, and had stood grouped together, even after they had called attention to themselves by Lord Ralles's shots. Cullen had to confess that he heard the whistle of the four bullets unpleasantly close.

"You have a right to be proud, Mr.

Cullen," I said. "You fellows did a tremendously plucky thing, and, thanks to you, we did n't lose anything."

"But you went to help too, Mr. Gordon," added Miss Cullen.

That made me color up, and, after a moment's hesitation, I said, —

"I'm not going to sail under false colors, Miss Cullen. When I went forward I did n't think I could do anything. I supposed whoever had pitched into the robbers was dead, and I expected to be the same inside of ten minutes."

"Then why did you risk your life," she asked, "if you thought it was useless?"

I laughed, and, though ashamed to tell it, replied, "I did n't want you to think that the Britishers had more pluck than I had."

She took my confession better than I hoped she would, laughing with me, and then said, "Well, that was courageous, after all."

"Yes," I confessed, "I was frightened into bravery."

"Perhaps if they had known the danger as well as you, they would have been less courageous," she continued; and I could have blessed her for the speech.

While we were still eating, the mail clerk came to my car and reported that the most careful search had failed to discover the three registered letters, and they had evidently been taken. This made me feel sober, slight as the probable loss was. He told me that his list showed they were all addressed to. Ash Forks, Arizona, making it improbable that their contents could be of any real value. If possible, I was more puzzled than ever.

At six-ten the runner whistled to show he had steam up. I told one of the brakemen to stay behind, and then went into 218. Mr. Cullen was still dressing, but I expressed my regrets through the door that I could not go with his party to the Grand Cañon, told him that all the stage arrangements had been completed, and promised to join him there in case my luck was good. Then I saw Frederic for a moment, to see how he was (for I had nearly forgotten him in the excitement), to find that he was gaining all the time, and preparing even to get up. When I returned to the saloon, the rest of the party were there, and I bade good-bye to the captain and Albert. Then I turned to Lord Ralles, and, holding out my hand, said, —

"Lord Ralles, I joked a little the other morning about the way you thought road agents ought to be treated. You have turned the joke very neatly and pluckily, and I want to apologize for myself and thank you for the railroad."

"Neither is necessary," he retorted airily, pretending not to see my hand.

I never claimed to have a good temper, and it was all I could do to hold myself in. I turned to Miss Cullen to wish her a pleasant trip, and the thought that this might be our last meeting made me forget even Lord Ralles.

"I hope it is n't good-bye, but only *au revoir*," she said. "Whether or no, you must let us see you some time in Chicago, so that I may show you how grateful I am for all the pleasure you have added to our trip." Then, as I stepped down off my platform, she leaned over the rail of 218, and added, in a low voice, " I thought you were just as brave as the rest, Mr. Gordon, and now I think you are braver."

I turned impulsively, and said, " You would think so, Miss Cullen, if you knew the sacrifice I am making." Then, without looking at her, I gave the signal, the bell rang, and No. 3 pulled off. The last thing I saw was a handkerchief waving off the platform of 218.

When the train dropped out of sight over a grade, I swallowed the lump in my throat and went to the telegraph instrument. I wired Coolidge to give the alarm to Fort Wingate, Fort Apache, Fort Thomas, Fort Grant, Fort Bayard, and Fort Whipple, though I thought the precaution a mere waste of energy. Then I sent the brakeman up to connect the cut wire.

" Two of the bullets struck up here, Mr. Gordon," the man called from the top of the pole.

" Surely not ! " I exclaimed.

" Yes, sir," he responded. " The bullet-holes are brand-new."

I took in the lay of the land, the embers of the fire showing me how the train had lain. " I don't wonder nobody was hit," I exclaimed, " if that's a sample of their shooting. Some one was a worse rattled man than I ever expect to be. Dig the bullets out, Douglas, so that we can have a look at them."

He brought them down in a minute. They proved to be Winchesters, as I had expected, for they were on the side from which the robbers must have fired.

" That chap must have been full of Arizona tangle-foot, to have fired as wild as he did," I ejaculated, and walked over to where the mail-car had stood, to see just how bad the shooting was. When I got there and faced about, it was really impossible to

believe any man could have done so badly,
for raising my own Winchester to the pole
put it twenty degrees out of range and nearly
forty degrees in the air. Yet there were the
cartridge-shells on the ground, to show that
I was in the place from which the shots had
been fired.

While I was still cogitating over this, the
special train I had ordered out from Flagstaff
came in sight, and in a few moments was
stopped where I was. It consisted of a
string of three flats and a box car, and brought
the sheriff, a dozen cowboys whom he had
sworn in as deputies, and their horses. I
was hopeful that with these fellows' greater
skill in such matters they could find what I
had not, but after a thorough examination of
the ground within a mile of the robbery they
were as much at fault as I had been.

"Them cusses must have a dugout nigh
abouts, for they could n't 'a' got away without
wings," the sheriff surmised.

I did n't put much stock in that idea, and
told the sheriff so.

" Waal, round up a better one," was his retort.

Not being able to do that, I told him of the bullets in the telegraph pole, and took him over to where the mail car had stood.

" Jerusalem crickets ! " was his comment as he measured the aim. " If that's where they put two of their pills, they must have pumped the other four inter the moon."

" What other four ? " I asked.

" Shots," he replied sententiously.

" The road agents only fired four times," I told him.

" Them and your pards must have been pretty nigh together for a minute, then," he said, pointing to the ground.

I glanced down, and sure enough, there were six empty cartridge-shells. I stood looking blankly at them, hardly able to believe what I saw; for Albert Cullen had said distinctly that the train-robbers had fired only four times, and that the last three Winchester shots I had heard had been fired by himself. Then, without speaking, I walked slowly back, searching along the edge of the road-bed for more shells ; but, though I went beyond the point where the last car had stood, not one did I find. Any man who has fired a Winchester knows that it drops its empty shell in loading, and I could therefore draw only one conclusion, — namely, that all seven discharges of the Winchesters had occurred up by the mail-car. I had heard of men supposing they had fired their guns through hearing another go off; but with a repeating rifle one has to fire before one can reload. The fact was evident that Albert Cullen either had fired his Winchester up by the mail-car, or else had not fired it at all. In either case he had lied, and Lord Ralles and Captain Ackland had backed him up in it.

CHAPTER V

A TRIP TO THE GRAND CAÑON

I STOOD pondering, for no explanation that would fit the facts seemed possible. I should have considered the young fellow's story only an attempt to gain a little reputation for pluck, if in any way I could have accounted for the appearance and disappearance of the robbers. Yet to suppose — which seemed the only other horn to the dilemma — that the son and guests of the vice-president of the Missouri Western, and one of our own directors, would be concerned in train-robbery was to believe something equally improbable. Indeed, I should have put the whole thing down as a practical joke of Mr. Cullen's party, if it had not been for the loss of the registered letters. Even a practical joker would hardly care to go to the length of cutting open government mail-pouches; for Uncle Sam does n't approve of such conduct.

Whatever the explanation, I had enough facts to prevent me from wasting more time on that alkali plain. Getting the men and horses back onto the cars, I jumped up on the tail-board and ordered the runner to pull out for Flagstaff. It was a run of seven hours, getting us in a little after eight, and in those hours I had done a lot of thinking which had all come to one result, — that Mr. Cullen's party was concerned in the hold-up.

The two private cars were on a siding, but the Cullens had left for the Grand Cañon the moment they had arrived, and were about reaching there by this time. I went to 218 and questioned the cook and waiter, but they had either seen nothing or else had been primed, for not a fact did I get from them. Going to my own car, I ordered a quick supper, and while I was eating it I questioned my boy. He told me that he had heard the shots, and had bolted the front door of my car, as I had ordered when I went out; that as he turned to go to a safer place, he had seen a man, revolver in hand, climb over the off-side gate of Mr. Cullen's car, and for a moment he had supposed it a road agent, till he saw that it was Albert Cullen.

" That was just after I had got off? " I asked.

" Yis, sah.

" Then it could n't have been Mr. Cullen, Jim," I declared, " for I found him up at the other end of the car."

" Tell you it wuz, Mr. Gordon," Jim insisted. " I done seen his face clar in de light, and he done go into Mr. Cullen's car whar de old gentleman wuz sittin'."

That set me whistling to myself, and I laughed to think how near I had come to giving nitroglycerin to a fellow who was only shamming heart-failure; for that it was Frederic Cullen who had climbed on the car I had n't the slightest doubt, the resemblance between the two brothers being quite strong enough to deceive any one who had never seen them together. I smiled a little, and remarked to myself, "I think I can make good my boast that I would catch the robbers; but whether the Cullens will like my doing it, I question. What is more, Lord Ralles will owe me a bottle." Then I thought of Madge, and did n't feel as pleased over my success as I had felt a moment before.

By nine o'clock the posse and I were in the saddle and skirting the San Francisco peaks. There was no use of pressing the ponies, for our game was n't trying to escape, and, for that matter, could n't, as the Colorado River was n't passable within fifty miles. It was a lovely moonlight night, and the ride through the pines was as pretty a one as I remember ever to have made. It set me thinking of Madge and of our talk the evening before, and of what a change twenty-four hours had brought. It was lucky I was riding an Indian pony, or I should probably have landed in a heap. I don't know that I should have cared particularly if a prairie-dog burrow had made me dash my brains out, for I was n't happy over the job that lay before me.

We watered at Silver Spring at quarter-past twelve. From that point we were clear of the pines and out on the plain, so we could go a better pace. This brought us to the half-way ranch by two, where we gave the ponies a feed and an hour's rest. We reached the last relay station just as the moon set, about three-forty; and, as all the rest of the ride was through coconino forest, we held up there for daylight, getting a little sleep meanwhile.

We rode into the camp at the Grand Cañon a little after eight, and the deserted look of the tents gave me a moment's fright, for I feared that the party had gone. Tolfree explained, however, that some had ridden out to Moran Point, and the rest had gone down Hance's trail. So I breakfasted and then took a look at Albert Cullen's chester. That it had been recently fired was as plain as the Grand Cañon itself; throwing back the bar, I found an empty cartridge shell, still oily from the discharge. That completed the tale of seven shots, I did n't feel absolutely safe till I had asked Tolfree if there had been any shooting of echoes by the party, but his denial rounded out my chain of evidence.

Telling the sheriff to guard the bags of the party carefully, I took two of the posse and rode over to Moran's Point. Sure enough, there were Mr. Cullen, Albert, and Captain Ackland. They gave a shout at seeing me, and even before I had reached them they called to know how I could come so soon, and if I had caught the robbers. Mr. Cullen started to tell his pleasure at my rejoining the party, but my expression made him pause, and it seemed to dawn on all three that the Winchester across my saddle, and the cowboys' hands resting nonchalantly on the revolvers in their belts, had a meaning.

" Mr. Cullen," I explained, " I 've got a

very unpleasant job on hand, which I don't want to make any worse than need be. Every fact points to your party as guilty of holding up the train last night and stealing those letters. Probably you were n't all concerned, but I've got to go on the assumption that you are all guilty, till you prove otherwise."

" Aw, you 're joking," drawled Albert.

"I hope so," I said, " but for the present I 've got to be English and treat the joke seriously."

" What do you want to do ? " asked Mr. Cullen.

" I don't wish to arrest you gentlemen unless you force me to," I said, " for I don't see that it will do any good. But I want you to return to camp with us."

They assented to that, and, single file, we rode back. When there I told each that he must be searched, to which they submitted at once. After that we went through their baggage. I was n't going to have the sheriff or cowboys tumbling over Miss Cullen's clothes, so I looked over her bag myself. The prettiness and daintiness of the various contents were a revelation to me, and I tried to put them back as neatly as I had found them, but I did n't know much about the articles, and it was a terrible job trying to fold up some of the things. Why, there was a big pink affair, lined with silk, with bits of ribbon and lace all over it, which nearly drove me out of my head, for I would have defied mortal man to pack it so that it should n't muss. I had a funny little feeling of tenderness for everything, which made fussing over it all a pleasure, even while I felt all the time that I was doing a sneak act and had really no right to touch her belongings. I did n't find anything incriminating, and the posse reported the same result with the other baggage. If the letters were still in existence, they were either concealed somewhere or were in the possession of the party in the Cañon. Telling the sheriff to keep those in the camp under absolute surveillance, I took a single man, and saddling a couple of mules, started down the trail.

We found Frederic and " Captain " Hance just dismounting at the Rock Cabin, and I told the former he was in custody for the present, and asked him where Miss Cullen and Lord Ralles were. He told me they were just behind; but I was n't going to take any risks, and, ordering the deputy to look after Cullen, I went on down the trail. I could n't resist calling back, —

" How 's your respiration, Mr. Cullen ? "

He laughed, and called, " Digitalis put me on my feet like a flash."

" He 's got the most brains of any man in this party," I remarked to myself.

The trail at this point is very winding, so that one can rarely see fifty feet in advance, and sometimes not ten. Owing to this, the first thing I knew I plumped round a curve on to a mule, which was patiently standing there. Just back of him was another, on which sat Miss Cullen, and standing close beside her was Lord Ralles. One of his

hands held the mule's bridle; the other held
Madge's arm, and he was saying, " You
owe it to me, and I will have one. Or
if — "

I swore to myself, and coughed aloud,
which made Miss Cullen look up. The
moment she saw me she cried, " Mr. Gordon ! How delightful ! " even while she
grew as red as she had been pale the moment before. Lord Ralles grew red too,
but in a different way.

" Have you caught the robbers ? " cried
Miss Cullen.

" I 'm afraid I have," I answered.

" What do you mean ? " she asked.

I smiled at the absolute innocence and
wonder with which she spoke, and replied,
" I know now, Miss Cullen, why you said I
was braver than the Britishers."

" How do you know ? "

I could n't resist getting in a side-shot at
Lord Ralles, who had mounted his mule and
sat scowling. " The train-robbers were such
thoroughgoing duffers at the trade," I said,

64

"that if they had left their names and addresses they would n't have made it much easier. We Americans may not know enough to deal with real road agents, but we can do something with amateurs."

"What are we stopping here for?" snapped Lord Ralles.

"I 'm sure I don't know," I responded. "Miss Cullen, if you will kindly pass us, and then if Lord Ralles will follow you, we will go on to the cabin. I must ask you to keep close together."

"I stay or go as I please, and not by your orders," asserted Lord Ralles, snappishly.

"Out in this part of the country," I said calmly, "it is considered shocking bad form for an unarmed man to argue with one who carries a repeating rifle. Kindly follow Miss Cullen." And, leaning over, I struck his mule with the loose ends of my bridle, starting it up the trail.

When we reached the cabin the deputy told me that he had made Frederic strip and had searched his clothing, finding nothing.

I ordered Lord Ralles to dismount and go into the cabin.

"For what ?" he demanded.

"We want to search you," I answered.

"I don't choose to be searched," he protested. "You have shown no warrant, nor — "

I wasn't in a mood towards him to listen to his talk. I swung my Winchester into line and announced, "I was sworn in last night as a deputy-sheriff, and am privileged to shoot a train-robber on sight. Either dead or alive, I'm going to search your clothing inside of ten minutes; and if you have no preference as to whether the examination is an ante- or post-mortem affair, I certainly haven't."

That brought him down off his high horse, — that is, mule, — and I sent the deputy in with him with directions to toss his clothes out to me, for I wanted to keep my eye on Miss Cullen and her brother, so as to prevent any legerdemain on their part.

One by one the garments came flying

through the door to me. As fast as I finished examining them I pitched them back,
except — Well, as I have thought it over
since then, I have decided that I did a mean
thing, and have regretted it. But just put
yourself in my place, and think of how Lord
Ralles had talked to me as if I was his servant, had refused my apology and thanks,
and been as generally " nasty " as he could,
and perhaps you won't blame me that, after
looking through his trousers, I gave them a
toss which, instead of sending them back
into the hut, sent them over the edge of the
trail. They went down six hundred feet
before they lodged in a poplar, and if his
lordship followed the trail he could get round
to them, but there would then be a hundred
feet of sheer rock between the trail and
the trousers. " I hope it will teach him to
study his Lord Chesterfield to better purpose,
for if politeness does n't cost anything, rude-
ness can cost considerable," I chuckled to
myself.

My amusement did not last long, for my

next thought was, " If those letters are concealed on any one, they are on Miss Cullen."
The thought made me lean up against my
mule, and turn hot and cold by turns.

A nice situation for a lover!

CHAPTER VI

THE HAPPENINGS DOWN HANCE'S TRAIL

MISS CULLEN was sitting on a rock apart from her brother and Hance, as I had asked her to do when I helped her dismount. I went over to where she sat, and said, boldly, —

"Miss Cullen, I want those letters."

"What letters?" she asked, looking me in the eyes with the most innocent of expressions. She made a mistake to do that, for I knew her innocence must be feigned, and so did n't put much faith in her face for the rest of the interview.

"And what is more," I continued, with a firmness of manner about as genuine as her innocence, "unless you will produce them at once, I shall have to search you."

"Mr. Gordon!" she exclaimed, but she put such surprise and grief and disbelief into

69

the four syllables that I wanted the earth to swallow me then and there.

"Why, Miss Cullen," I cried, "look at my position. I'm being paid to do certain things, and — "

"But that need n't prevent your being a gentleman," she interrupted.

That made me almost desperate. "Miss Cullen," I groaned, hurriedly, "I'd rather be burned alive than do what I've got to, but if you won't give me those letters, search you I must."

"But how can I give you what I have n't?" she cried, indignantly, assuming again her innocent expression.

"Will you give me your word of honor that those letters are not concealed in your clothes?"

"I will," she answered.

I was very much taken aback, for it would have been so easy for Miss Cullen to have said so before that I had become convinced she must have them.

"And do you give me your word?"

"I do," she affirmed, but she did n't look me in the face as she said it.

I ought to have been satisfied, but I was n't, for, in spite of her denial, something forced me still to believe she had them, and looking back now, I think it was her manner. I stood reflecting for a minute, and then requested, "Please stay where you are for a moment." Leaving her, I went over to Fred.

"Mr. Cullen," I said, "Miss Cullen, rather than be searched, has acknowledged that she has the letters, and says that if we men will go into the hut she 'll get them for me."

He rose at once. "I told my father not to drag her in," he muttered, sadly. "I don't care about myself, Mr. Gordon, but can't you keep her out of it? She 's as innocent of any real wrong as the day she was born."

"I 'll do everything in my power," I promised. Then he and Hance went into the cabin, and I walked back to the culprit.

"Miss Cullen," I said, gravely, "you have those letters, and must give them to me."

"But I told you —" she began.

To spare her a second untruth, I interrupted her by saying, "I trapped your brother into acknowledging that you have them."

"You must have misunderstood him," she replied, calmly, "or else he did n't know that the arrangement was changed."

Her steadiness rather shook my conviction, but I said, "You must give me those letters, or I must search you."

"You never would!" she cried, rising and looking me in the face.

On impulse I tried a big bluff. I took hold of the lapel of her waist, intending to undo just one button. I let go in fright when I found there was no button,—only an awful complication of hooks or some other feminine method for keeping things together,—and I grew red and trembled, thinking what might have happened had I, by bad luck, made anything come undone. If Miss Cullen had been noticing me, she would have seen a terribly scared man.

But she was n't, luckily, for the moment my hand touched her dress, and before she could realize that I snatched it away, she collapsed on the rock, and burst into tears. "Oh! oh!" she sobbed, "I begged papa not to, but he insisted they were safest with me. I'll give them to you, if you'll only go away and not — " Her tears made her inarticulate, and without waiting for more I ran into the hut, feeling as near like a murderer as a guiltless man could.

Lord Ralles by this time was making almost as much noise as an engine pulling a heavy freight up grade under forced draft, swearing over his trousers, and was offering the cowboy and Hance money to recover them. When they told him this was impossible he tried to get them to sell or hire a pair, but they did n't like the idea of riding into camp minus those essentials any better than he did. While I waited they settled the difficulty by

strapping a blanket round him, and by splitting it up the middle and using plenty of cord
they rigged him out after a fashion; but I
think if he could have seen himself and been
given an option he would have preferred to
wait till it was dark enough to creep into
camp unnoticed.

Before long Miss Cullen called, and when
I went to her she handed me, without a
word, three letters. As she did so she crim-
soned violently, and looked down in her
mortification. I was so sorry for her that,
though a moment before I had been judging
her harshly, I now could n't help saying, —

" Our positions have been so difficult,
Miss Cullen, that I don't think we either of
us are quite responsible for our actions."

She said nothing, and, after a pause, I
continued, —

" I hope you'll think as leniently of my
conduct as you can, for I can't tell you how
grieved I am to have pained you."

Cullen joined us at this point, and, knowing that every moment we remained would

be distressing to his sister, I announced that we would start up the trail. I had n't the heart to offer to help her mount, and after Frederic had put her up we fell into single file behind Hance, Lord Ralles coming last.

As soon as we started I took a look at the three letters. They were all addressed to Theodore E. Camp, Esq., Ash Forks, Arizona, — one of the directors of the K. & A. and also of the Great Southern. With this clue, for the first time things began to clear up to me, and when the trail broadened enough to permit it, I pushed my mule up alongside of Cullen and asked, —

" The letters contain proxies for the K. & A. election next Friday ? "

He nodded his head. " The Missouri Western and the Great Southern are fighting for control," he explained, " and we should have won but for three blocks of Eastern stock that had promised their proxies to the G. S. Rather than lose the fight, we arranged to learn when those proxies were mailed, — that was what kept me behind, —

and then to hold up the train that carried them."

" Was it worth the risk ? " I ejaculated.

" If we had succeeded, yes. My father had put more than was safe into Missouri Western and into California Central. The G. S. wants control to end the traffic agreements, and that means bankruptcy to my father."

I nodded, seeing it all as clear as day, and hardly blaming the Cullens for what they had done; for any one who has had dealings with the G. S. is driven to pretty desperate methods to keep from being crushed, and when one is fighting an antagonist that won't regard the law, or rather one that, through control of legislatures and judges, makes the law to suit its needs, the temptation is strong to use the same weapons one's self.

" The toughest part of it is," Fred went on, " that we thought we had the whole thing ' hands down,' and that was what made my father go in so deep. Only the death of one of the M. W. directors, who held eight thousand shares of K. & A., got us in this hole, for the G. S. put up a relation to contest the will, and so delayed the obtaining of letters of administration, blocking his executors from giving a proxy. It was as mean a trick as ever was played."

"The G. S. is a tough customer to fight," I remarked, and asked, "Why did n't you burn the letters?" really wishing they had done so.

"We feared duplicate proxies might get through in time, and thought that by keeping these we might cook up a question as to which were legal, and then by injunction prevent the use of either."

"And those Englishmen," I inquired, "are they real?"

"Oh, certainly," he rejoined. "They were visiting my brother, and thought the whole thing great larks." Then he told me how the thing had been done. They had sent Miss Cullen to my car, so as to get me out of the way, though she had n't known it. He and his brother got off the train at the last stop, with the guns and' masks, and concealed themselves on the platform of the mail-car. Here they had been joined by the Britishers at the right moment, the disguises assumed, and the train held up as already told. Of course the dynamite cartridge was only a blind, and the letters had been thrown about the car merely to confuse the clerk. Then while Frederic Cullen, with the letters, had stolen back to the car, the two Englishmen had crept back to where they had stood. Here, as had been arranged, they opened fire, which Albert Cullen duly returned, and then joined them. "I don't see now how you spotted us," Frederic ended.

I told him, and his disgust was amusing to see. "Going to Oxford may be all right for the classics," he growled, "but it's destructive to gumption."

We rode into camp a pretty gloomy crowd, and those of the party waiting for us there were not much better; but when Lord Ralles dismounted and showed up in his substitute for trousers there was a general shout of laughter. Even Miss Cullen had to laugh for a moment. And as his lordship bolted for his tent, I said to myself, " Honors are easy."

I told the sheriff that I had recovered the lost property, but did not think any arrests necessary as yet; and, as he was the agent of the K. & A. at Flagstaff, he did n't question my opinion. I ordered the stage out, and told Tolfree to give us a feed before we started, but a more silent meal I never sat down to, and I noticed that Miss Cullen did n't eat anything, while the tragic look on her face was so pathetic as nearly to drive me frantic.

We started a little after five, and were clear of the timber before it was too dark to see. At the relay station we waited an hour for the moon, after which it was a clear track. We reached the half-way ranch about eleven, and while changing the stage horses I roused Mrs. Klostermeyer, and succeeded in getting enough cold mutton and bread to make two rather decent-looking sandwiches.

With these and a glass of whiskey and water I went to the stage, to find Miss Cullen curled up on the seat asleep, her head resting in her brother's arms.

" She has nearly worried herself to death ever since you told her that road agents were hung," Frederic whispered; " and she's been crying to-night over that lie she told you, and altogether she's worn out with travel and excitement."

I screwed the cover on the travelling-glass, and put it with the sandwiches in the bottom of the stage. " It's a long and a rough ride," I said, " and if she wakes up they may give her a little strength. I only wish I could have spared her the fatigue and anxiety."

" She thought she had to lie for father's sake, but she's nearly broken-hearted over it," he continued.

I looked Frederic in the face as I said, " I honor her for it," and in that moment he and I became friends.

" Just see how pretty she is ! " he whispered, with evident affection and pride, turning back the flap of the rug in which she was wrapped.

She was breathing gently, and there was just that touch of weariness and sadness in her face that would appeal to any man. It made me gulp, I'm proud to say; and when I was back on my pony, I said to myself, "For her sake, I'll pull the Cullens out of this scrape, if it costs me my position."

CHAPTER VII

A CHANGE OF BASE

WE did not reach Flagstaff till seven, and I told the stage-load to take possession of their car, while I went to my own. It took me some time to get freshened up, and then I ate my breakfast; for after riding seventy-two miles in one night even the most heroic purposes have to take the side-track. I think, as it was, I proved my devotion pretty well by not going to sleep, since I had been up three nights, with only such naps as I could steal in the saddle, and had ridden over a hundred and fifty miles to boot. But I couldn't bear to think of Miss Cullen's anxiety, and the moment I had made myself decent, and finished eating, I went into 218.

The party were all in the dining-room, but it was a very different-looking crowd from the one with which that first breakfast had been eaten, and they all looked at me as I entered as if I were the executioner come for victims.

"Mr. Cullen," I began, "I've been forced to do a lot of things that were n't pleasant, but I don't want to do more than I need. You're not the ordinary kind of road agents, and, as I presume your address is known, I don't see any need of arresting one of our own directors as yet. All I ask is that you give me your word, for the party, that none of you will try to leave the country."

"Certainly, Mr. Gordon," he responded. "And I thank you for your great consideration."

"I shall have to report the case to our president, and, I suppose, to the Postmaster-General, but I sha'n't hurry about either. What they will do, I can't say. Probably you know how far you can keep them quiet."

"I think the local authorities are all I have to fear, provided time is given me."

" I have dismissed the sheriff and his posse, and I gave them a hundred dollars for their work, and three bottles of pretty good whiskey I had on my car. Unless they get orders from elsewhere, you will not hear any further from them."

" You must let me reimburse what expense we have put you to, Mr. Gordon. I only wish I could as easily repay your kindness."

Nodding my head in assent, as well as in recognition of his thanks, I continued, " It was my duty, as an official of the K. & A., to recover the stolen mail, and I had to do it."

" We understand that," said Mr. Cullen, " and do not for a moment blame you."

" But," I went on, for the first time looking at Madge, " it is not my duty to take part in a contest for control of the K. & A., and I shall therefore act in this case as I should in any other loss of mail."

" And that is — ? " asked Frederic.

"I am about to telegraph for instructions from Washington," I replied. "As the G. S. by trickery has dishonestly tied up some of your proxies, they ought not to object if we do the same by honest means; and I think I can manage so that Uncle Sam will prevent those proxies from being voted at Ash Forks on Friday."

If a galvanic battery had been applied to the group about the breakfast table, it would n't have made a bigger change. Madge clapped her hands in joy; Mr. Cullen said " God bless you ! " with real feeling; Frederic jumped up and slapped me on the shoulder, crying, " Gordon, you 're the biggest old trump breathing ; " while Albert and the captain shook hands with each other, in evident jubilation. Only Lord Ralles remained passive.

" Have you breakfasted ? " asked Mr. Cullen, when the first joy was over.

" Yes," I said. " I only stopped in on my way to the station to telegraph the Postmaster-General."

"May I come with you and see what you say?" cried Fred, jumping up.

I nodded, and Miss Cullen said, questioningly, "Me too!" making me very happy by the question, for it showed that she would speak to me. I gave an assent quite as eagerly and in a moment we were all walking towards the platform. Despite Lord Ralles, I felt happy, and especially as I had not dreamed that she would ever forgive me.

I took a telegraph blank, and, putting it so that Miss Cullen could see what I said, wrote, —

"Postmaster-General, Washington, D. C. I hold, awaiting your instructions, the three registered letters stolen from No. 3 Overland Missouri Western Express on Monday, October fourteenth, loss of which has already been notified you."

Then I paused and said, "So far, that's routine, Miss Cullen. Now comes the help for you," and I continued : —

"The letters may have been tampered

with, and I recommend a special agent. Reply Flagstaff, Arizona. Richard Gordon, Superintendent K. & A. R. R."

"What will that do?" she asked.

"I'm not much at prophecy, and we'll wait for the reply," I said.

All that day we lay at Flagstaff, and after a good sleep, as there was no use keeping the party cooped up in their car, I drummed up some ponies and took the Cullens and Ackland over to the Indian cliff-dwellings. I don't think Lord Ralles gained anything by staying behind in a sulk, for it was a very jolly ride, or at least that was what it was to me. I had of course to tell them all how I had settled on them as the criminals, and a general history of my doings. To hear Miss Cullen talk, one would have inferred I was the greatest of living detectives.

"The mistake we made," she asserted, "was not securing Mr. Gordon's help to begin with, for then we should never have needed to hold the train up, or if we had we should never have been discovered."

What was more to me than this ill-deserved admiration were two things she said on the way back, when we two had paired off and were a bit behind the rest.

"The sandwiches and the whiskey were very good," she told me, "and I'm so grateful for the trouble you took."

"It was a pleasure," I said.

"And, Mr. Gordon," she continued, and then hesitated for a moment, — "my — Frederic told me that you — you said you honored me for — ?"

"I do," I exclaimed energetically, as she paused and colored.

"Do you really?" she cried. "I thought Fred was only trying to make me less unhappy by saying that you did."

"I said it, and I meant it," I told her.

"I have been so miserable over that lie," she went on; "but I thought if I let you have the letters it would ruin papa. I really would n't mind poverty myself, Mr. Gordon, but he takes such pride in success that I could n't be the one to do it. And then, after you told me that train-robbers were hung, I had to lie to save them. I ought to have known you would help us."

I thought this a pretty good time to make a real apology for my conduct on the trail, as well as to tell her how sorry I was at not having been able to repack her bag better. She accepted my apology very sweetly, and assured me her belongings had been put away so neatly that she had wondered who did it. I knew she only said this out of kindness, and told her so, telling also of my struggles over that pink-beribboned and belaced affair, in a way which made her laugh. I had thought it was a ball gown, and wondered at her taking it to the Cañon ; but she explained that it was what she called a " throw " — which I told her accounted for the throes I had gone through over it. It made me open my eyes, thinking that anything so pretty could be used for the same purposes for which I use my crash bath-gown, and while my eyes were open I saw the folly of thinking that a girl who wore such things would, or in fact could, ever get along on my salary. In that way the incident was a good lesson for me, for it made me feel that, even if there had been no Lord Ralles, I still should have had no chance.

On our return to the cars there was a telegram from the Postmaster-General awaiting me. After a glance at it, as the rest of the party looked anxiously on, I passed it over to Miss Cullen, for I wanted her to have the triumph of reading it aloud to them. It read, —

"Hold letters pending arrival of special agent Jackson, due in Flagstaff October twentieth."

"The election is the eighteenth," Frederic laughed, executing a war dance on the platform. "The G. S.'s dough is cooked."

"I must waltz with some one," cried Madge, and before I could offer she took hold of Albert and the two went whirling about, much to my envy. The Cullens were about the most jubilant road agents I had ever seen.

After consultation with Mr. Cullen, we had 218 and 97 attached to No. 1 when it arrived, and started for Ash Forks. He wanted to be on the ground a day in advance, and I could easily be back in Flagstaff before the arrival of the special agent.

I took dinner in 218, and they toasted me, as if I had done something heroic instead of merely having sent a telegram. Later four sat down to poker, while Miss Cullen, Fred, and I went out and sat on the platform of the car while Madge played on her guitar and sang to us. She had a very sweet voice, and before she had been singing long we had the crew of a " dust express " — as we jokingly call a gravel train — standing about, and they were speedily reinforced by many cowboys, who deserted the medley of cracked pianos or accordions of the Western saloons to listen to her, and who, not being over-careful in the terms with which they expressed their approval, finally by their riotous admiration drove us inside. At Miss Cullen's suggestion we three had a second game of poker, but with chips and not money. She was an awfully reckless player, and the luck was dead in my favor, so Madge kept borrowing my chips, till she was so deep in that we both lost account. Finally, when we parted for the night she held out her hand, and, in the prettiest of ways, said, —

"I am so deeply in your debt, Mr. Gordon, that I don't see how I can ever repay you."

I tried to think of something worth saying, but the words would n't come, and I could only shake her hand. But, duffer as I was, the way she had said those words, and the double meaning she had given them, would have made me the happiest fellow alive if I could only have forgotten the existence of Lord Ralles.

CHAPTER VIII

HOW DID THE SECRET LEAK OUT?

I MADE up for my three nights' lack of
sleep by not waking the next morning till
after ten. When I went to 218, I found
only the *chef*, and he told me the party had
gone for a ride. Since I could n't talk to
Madge, I went to work at my desk, for
I had been rather neglecting my routine
work. While I still wrote, I heard horses'
hoofs, and, looking up, saw the Cullens returning. I went out on the platform to wish
them good-morning, arriving just in time to
see Lord Ralles help Miss Cullen out of
her saddle; and the way he did it, and the
way he continued to hold her hand after
she was down, while he said something to
her, made me grit my teeth and look the

93

other way.   None of the riders had seen me, so I slipped into my car and went back to work.   Fred came in presently to see if I was up yet, and to ask me to lunch, but I felt so miserable and down-hearted that I made an excuse of my late breakfast for not joining them.

After luncheon 'the party in the other special all came out and walked up and down the platform, the sound of their voices and laughter only making me feel the bluer. Before long I heard a rap on one of my windows, and there was Miss Cullen peering in at me. The moment I looked up, she called, —

" Won't you make one of us, Mr. Misan-thrope ? "

I called myself all sorts of a fool, but out I went as eagerly as if there had been some hope.   Miss Cullen began to tease me over my sudden access of energy, declaring that she was sure it was a pose for their benefit, or else due to a guilty conscience over having slept so late.

" I hoped you would ride with us, though

perhaps it would n't have paid you. Apparently there is nothing to see in Ash Forks."

" There is something that may interest you all," I suggested, pointing to a special that had been dropped off No. 2 that morning.

" What is it ? " asked Madge.

" It 's a G. S. special," I said, " and Mr. Camp and Mr. Baldwin and two G. S. officials came in on it."

" What do you think he 'd give for those letters ? " laughed Fred.

" If they were worth so much to you, I suppose they can't be worth any less to the G. S.," I replied.

" Fortunately, there is no way that he can learn where they are," said Mr. Cullen.

" Don't let 's stand still," cried Miss Cullen. " Mr. Gordon, I 'll run you a race to the end of the platform." She said this only after getting a big lead, and she got there about eight inches ahead of me, which pleased her mightily. " It takes men so

long to get started," was the way she explained her victory. Then she walked me
beyond the end of the boarding to explain
the workings of a switch to her. That it
was only a pretext she proved to me the
moment I had relocked the bar, by saying, —

"Mr. Gordon, may I ask you a question?"

"Certainly," I assented.

"It is one I should ask papa or Fred,
but I am afraid they might not tell me the
truth. You will, won't you?" she begged,
very earnestly.

"I will," I promised.

"Supposing," she continued, "that it became known that you have those letters?
Would it do our side any harm?"

I thought for a moment, and then shook
my head. "No new proxies could arrive
here in time for the election," I said, "and
the ones I have will not be voted."

She still looked doubtful, and asked,
"Then why did papa say just now, 'Fortunately'?"

"He merely meant that it was safer they should n't know."

"Then it is better to keep it a secret?" she asked, anxiously.

"I suppose so," I said, and then added, "Why should you be afraid of asking your father?"

"Because he might — well, if he knew, I'm sure he would sacrifice himself; and I could n't run the risk."

"I am afraid I don't understand?" I questioned.

"I would rather not explain," she said, and of course that ended the subject.

Our exercise taken, we went back to the Cullens' car, and Madge left us to write some letters. A moment later Lord Ralles remembered he had not written home recently, and he too went forward to the dining-room. That made me call myself — something, for not having offered Miss Cullen the use of my desk in 97. Owing to this the two missed part of the big game we were playing; for barely were they gone when one of the servants brought a card to Mr. Cullen, who looked at it and exclaimed, "Mr. Camp!" Then, after a speaking pause, in which we all exchanged glances, he said, "Bring him in."

On Mr. Camp's entrance he looked as much surprised as we had all done a moment before. "I beg your pardon for intruding, Mr. Cullen," he said. "I was told that this was Mr. Gordon's car, and I wish to see him."

"I am Mr. Gordon."

"You are travelling with Mr. Cullen?" he inquired, with a touch of suspicion in his manner.

"No," I answered. "My special is the next car, and I was merely enjoying a cigar here."

"Ah!" said Mr. Camp. "Then I won't interrupt your smoke, and will only relieve you of those letters of mine."

I took a good pull at my cigar, and blew the smoke out in a cloud slowly to gain time. "I don't think I follow you," I said.

" I understand that you have in your possession three letters addressed to me."

" I have," I assented.

" Then I will ask you to deliver them to me."

" I can't do that."

" Why not ?" he challenged. " They 're my property."

I produced the Postmaster-General's telegram and read it to him.

" Why, this is infamous !" Mr. Camp cried. " What use will those letters be after the eighteenth ? It 's a conspiracy."

" I can only obey instructions," I said.

" It shall cost you your position if you do," Mr. Camp threatened.

As I 've already said, I have n't a good temper, and when he told me that I could n't help retorting, —

" That 's quite on a par with most G. S. methods."

" I 'm not speaking for the G. S., young man," roared Mr. Camp. "I speak as a director of the Kansas & Arizona. What is more, I will have those letters inside of twenty-four hours."

He made an angry exit, and I said to Fred, " I wish you would stroll about and spy out the proceedings of the enemy's camp. He may telegraph to Washington, an if there's any chance of the Postmaster-General revoking his order I must go back to Flagstaff on No. 4 this afternoon."

" He sha'n't do anything that I don't know about till he goes to bed," Fred promised. " But how the deuce did he know that you had those letters ? "

That was just what we were all puzzling over, for only the occupants of No. 218 and myself, so far as I knew, were in a position to let Mr. Camp hear of that fact.

As Fred made his exit he said, " Don't tell Madge that there is a new complication, for the dear girl has had worries enough already."

Miss Cullen not rejoining us, and Lord Ralles presently doing so, I went to my own car, for he and I were not good furniture for the same room. Before I had been there long, Fred came rushing in.

" Camp and Baldwin have been in consultation with a lawyer," he said, "and now the three have just boarded those cars," pointing out the window at the branch-line train that was to leave for Phœnix in two minutes.

" You must go with them," I urged, " and keep us informed as to what they do, for they evidently are going to set the law on us, and the G. S. has always owned the Territorial judges, so they 'll stretch a point to oblige them."

" Have I time to fill a bag ? "

" Plenty," I assured him, and, going out, I ordered the train held till I should give the word.

" What does it all mean ? " asked Miss Cullen, joining me.

I laughed, and replied, " I 'm doing a braver thing even than your party did ; I 'm holding up a train all by my lonesome."

" But my brother came dashing in just now and said he was starting for Phœnix."

"Let her go," I called to the conductor, as Fred jumped aboard; and the train pulled out.

"I hope there's nothing wrong?" Madge questioned, anxiously.

"Nothing to worry over," I laughed. "Only a little more fun for our money. By the way, Miss Cullen," I went on, to avoid her questions, "if you have your letters ready, and will let me have them at once, I can get them on No. 4, so that they'll go East to-night."

Miss Cullen blushed as if I had said something I ought not to have, and stammered, "I — I changed my mind, and — that is — I didn't write them, after all."

"I beg your pardon, — I ought to have known; I mean, it's very natural," I faltered and stuttered, thinking what a dunce I had been not to understand that both hers and Lord Ralles's letters had been only a pretext to get away from the rest of us.

My blundering apology and evident embarrassment deepened Miss Cullen's blush fivefold, and she explained, hurriedly, "I found

I was tired, and so, instead of writing, I went to my room and rested."

I suppose any girl would have invented the same yarn, yet it hurt me more than the bigger one she had told on Hance's trail. Small as the incident was, it made me very blue, and led me to shut myself up in my own car for the rest of that afternoon and evening. Indeed, I could n't sleep, but sat up working, quite forgetful of the passing hours, till a glance at my watch startled me with the fact that it was a quarter of two. Feeling like anything more than sleep, I went out on the platform, and, lighting a cigar, paced up and down, thinking of — well, thinking.

The night agent was sitting in the station, nodding, and after I had walked for an hour I went in to ask him if the train to Phœnix had arrived on time. Just as I opened the door, the telegraph instrument began clicking, and called Ash Forks. The man, with the curious ability that operators get of recognizing their own call, even in sleep, waked up instantly and responded, and, not wishing to interrupt him, I delayed asking my question till he should be free. I stood there thinking of Madge, and listening heedlessly as the instrument ticked off the cipher signature of the sending operator, and the " twenty-four paid." But as I heard the clicks .... which meant ph, I suddenly became attentive, and when it completed " Phœnix "I concluded Fred was wiring me, and listened for what followed the date. This is what the instrument ticked : —

That may not look particularly intelligible, but if the Phœnix operator had been talking over the 'phone to me he could n't have said any plainer, —

" Sheriff yavapai county ash forks arizona be at rail road station three forty five today to meet train arriving from phœnix prepared to immediately serve peremptory mandamus issued tonight by judge wilson sig theodore e camp."

My question being pretty thoroughly answered, I went back and continued my walk; but before five minutes had passed, the operator came out, and handed me a message. It was from Fred, and read thus: —

" Camp, Baldwin, and lawyer went at once to house of Judge Wilson, where they stayed an hour. They then returned with judge to station, and after despatching a telegram have taken seats in train for Ash Forks, leaving here at three twenty-five. I shall return with them."

A bigger idiot than I could have understood the move. I was to be hauled before

Judge Wilson by means of mandamus proceedings, and, as he was notoriously a G. S.
judge, and was coming to Ash Forks solely
to oblige Mr. Camp, he would unquestion-
ably declare the letters the property of Mr.
Camp and order their delivery.

Apparently I had my choice of being a
traitor to Madge, of going to prison for contempt of court, or of running away, which
was not far off from acknowledging that I
had done something wrong. I did n't like
any one of the options.

CHAPTER IX

A TALK BEFORE BREAKFAST

LOOKING at my watch, I found it was a little after three, which meant six in Washington: allowing for transmission, a telegram would reach there in time to be on hand with the opening of the Departments. I therefore wired at once to the following effect : —

"Postmaster-General, Washington, D.C. A peremptory mandamus has been issued by Territorial judge to compel me to deliver to addressee the three registered letters which by your directions, issued October sixteenth, I was to hold pending arrival of special agent Jackson. Service of writ will be made at three forty-five to-day unless prevented. Telegraph me instructions how to act."

That done I had a good tub, took a brisk walk down the track, and felt so freshened up as to be none the worse for my sleepless night. I returned to the station a little after six, and, to my surprise, found Miss Cullen walking up and down the platform.

"You are up early!" we both said together.

"Yes," she sighed. "I could n't sleep last night."

"You 're not unwell, I hope?"

"No, — except mentally."

I looked a question, and she went on: "I have some worries, and then last night I saw you were all keeping some bad news from me, and so I could n't sleep."

"Then we did wrong to make a mystery of it, Miss Cullen," I said, "for it really is n't anything to trouble about. Mr. Camp is simply taking legal steps to try to force me to deliver those letters to him."

"And can he succeed?"

"No."

"How will you stop him?"

"I don't know yet just what we shall do, but if worse comes to worse I will allow myself to be committed for contempt of court."

" What would they do with you ? "

" Give me free board for a time."

" Not send you to prison ? "

" Yes."

" Oh ! " she cried, " that must n't be. You must not make such a sacrifice for us."

" I 'd do more than that for *you*," I said, and I could n't help putting a little emphasis on the last word, though I knew I had no right to do it.

She understood me, and blushed rosily, even while she protested, " It is too much — "

" There 's really no likelihood," I interrupted, " of my being able to assume a martyr's crown, Miss Cullen ; so don't begin to pity me till I 'm behind the bars."

" But I can't bear to think — "

" Don't," I interrupted again, rejoicing all the time at her evident anxiety, and blessing my stars for the luck they had brought me. " Why, Miss Cullen," I went on, " I 've become so interested in your success and the licking of those fellows that I really think I'd stand about anything rather than that they should win. Yesterday, when Mr. Camp threatened to —" Then I stopped, as it suddenly occurred to me that it was best not to tell Madge that I might lose my position, for it would look like a kind of bid for her favor, and, besides, would only add to her worries.

"Threatened what?" asked Miss Cullen.

"Threatened to lose his temper," I answered.

"You know that was n't what you were going to say," Madge said reproachfully.

"No, it was n't," I laughed.

"Then what was it?"

"Nothing worth speaking about."

"But I want to know what he threatened."

"Really, Miss Cullen," I began; but she interrupted me by saying anxiously, —

"He can't hurt papa, can he?"

"No," I replied.

"Or my brothers?"

"He can't touch any of them without

my help. And he'll have work to get that, I suspect."

"Then why can't you tell me?" demanded Miss Cullen. "Your refusal makes me think you are keeping back some danger to them."

"Why, Miss Cullen," I said, "I did n't like to tell his threat, because it seemed — well, I may be wrong, but I thought it might look like an attempt — an appeal — Oh, pshaw!" I faltered, like a donkey, — "I can't say it as I want to put it."

"Then tell me right out what he threatened," begged Madge.

"He threatened to get me discharged."

That made Madge look very sober, and for a moment there was silence. Then she said, —

"I never thought of what you were risking to help us, Mr. Gordon. And I 'm afraid it 's too late to — "

"Don't worry about me," I hastened to interject. "I 'm a long way from being discharged, and, even if I should be, Miss

Cullen, I know my business, and it won't be long before I have another place."

"But it's terrible to think of the injury we may have caused you," sighed Madge, sadly. "It makes me hate the thought of money."

"That's a very poor thing to hate," I said, "except the lack of it."

"Are you so anxious to get rich?" asked Madge, looking up at me quickly, as we walked, — for we had been pacing up and down the platform during our chat.

"I haven't been till lately."

"And what made you change?" she questioned.

"Well," I said, fishing round for some reason other than the true one, "perhaps I want to take a rest."

"You are the worst man for fibs I ever knew," she laughed.

I felt myself getting red, while I ex claimed, "Why, Miss Cullen, I never set up for a George Washington, but I don't think I'm a bit worse liar than nine men in —"

" Oh," she cried, interrupting me, " I did n't mean that way. I meant that when you try to fib you always do it so badly that one sees right through you. Now, acknowledge that you would n't stop work if you could ? "

" Well, no, I would n't," I owned up. " The truth is, Miss Cullen, that I'd like to be rich, because — well, hang it, I don't care if I do say it — because I'm in love."

Madge laughed at my confusion, and asked, " With money ? "

" No," I said. " With just the nicest, sweetest, prettiest girl in the world."

Madge took a look at me out of the corner of her eye, and remarked, " It must be breakfast time."

Considering that it was about six-thirty, I wanted to ask who was telling a taradiddle now ; but I resisted the temptation, and replied, —

" No. And I promise not to bother you about my private affairs any more."

Madge laughed again merrily, saying,

"You are the most obvious man I ever met. Now why did you say that?"

"I thought you were making breakfast an excuse," I said, "because you did n't like the subject."

"Yes, I was," said Madge, frankly. "Tell me about the girl you are engaged to."

I was so taken aback that I stopped in my walk, and merely looked at her.

"For instance," she asked coolly, when she saw that I was speechless, "what does she look like?"

"Like, like—" I stammered, still embarrassed by this bold carrying of the war into my own camp,—"like an angel."

"Oh," said Madge, eagerly, "I 've always wanted to know what angels were like. Describe her to me."

"Well," I said, getting my second wind, so to speak, "she has the bluest eyes I 've ever seen. Why, Miss Cullen, you said you 'd never seen anything so blue as the sky yesterday; but even the atmosphere of 'rainless Arizona' has to take a back seat when her eyes are round. And they are just like the atmosphere out here. You can look into them for a hundred miles, but you can't get to the bottom."

" The Arizona sky is wonderful," said Madge. " How do the scientists account for it ? "

I was n't going to have my description of Miss Cullen side-tracked, for, since she had given me the chance, I wanted her to know just what I thought of her. Therefore I did n't follow lead on the Arizona skies, but went on, —

" And I really think her hair is just as beautiful as her eyes. It 's light brown, very curly, and — "

" Her complexion ! " exclaimed Madge. " Is she a mulatto ? And, if so, how can a complexion be curly ? "

" Her complexion," I said, not a bit rattled, " is another great beauty of hers. She has one of those skins — "

" Furs are out of fashion at present," she interjected, laughing wickedly.

"Now look here, Miss Cullen," I cried, indignantly, " I'm not going to let even you make fun of her."

"I can't help it," she laughed, "when you look so serious and intense."

"It's something I feel intense about, Miss Cullen," I said, not a little pained, I confess, at the way she was joking. I don't mind a bit being laughed at, but Miss Cullen knew, about as well as I, whom I was talking about, and it seemed to me she was laughing at my love for her. Under this impression I went on, "I suppose it is funny to you; probably so many men have been in love with you that a man's love for a woman has come to mean very little in your eyes. But out here we don't make a joke of love, and when we care for a woman we care — well, it's not to be put in words, Miss Cullen."

"I really did n't mean to hurt your feelings, Mr. Gordon," said Madge, gently, and quite serious now. "I ought not to have tried to tease you."

"There!" I said, my irritation entirely

gone. "I had no right to lose my temper, and I'm sorry I spoke so unkindly. The truth is, Miss Cullen, the girl I care for is in love with another man, and so I'm bitter and ill-natured in these days."

My companion stopped walking at the steps of 218, and asked, "Has she told you so?"

"No," I answered. "But it's as plain as she's pretty."

Madge ran up the steps and opened the door of the car. As she turned to close it, she looked down at me with the oddest of expressions, and said, —

"How dreadfully ugly she must be!"

CHAPTER X

WAITING FOR HELP

IF ever a fellow was bewildered by a single speech, it was Richard Gordon. I walked up and down that platform till I was called to breakfast, trying to decide what Miss Cullen had meant to express, only to succeed in reading fifty different meanings into her parting six words. I wanted to think that it was her way of suggesting that I deceived myself in thinking that there was anything between Lord Ralles and herself; but, though I wished to believe this, I had seen too much to the contrary to take stock in the idea. Yet I could n't believe that Madge was a coquette; I became angry and hot with myself for even thinking it for a moment.

Puzzle as I did over the words, I managed to eat a good breakfast, and then went into the Cullens' car and electrified the party by telling them of Camp's and Fred's despatches, and how I had come to overhear the former. Mr. Cullen and Albert could n't say enough about my cleverness in what had really been pure luck, and seemed to think I had sat up all night in order to hear that telegram. The person for whose opinion I cared the most — Miss Cullen — did n't say anything, but she gave me a look that set my heart beating like a trip-hammer and made me put the most hopeful construction on that speech of hers. It seemed impossible that she did n't care for Lord Ralles, and that she might care for me; but, after having had no hope whatsoever, the smallest crumb of a chance nearly lifted me off my feet.

We had a consultation over what was best to be done, but did n't reach any definite conclusion till the station-agent brought me a telegram from the Postmaster-General. Breaking it open, I read aloud, —

" Do not allow service of writ, and retain possession of letters according to prior in-

structions. At the request of this department, the Secretary of War has directed the
commanding officer at Fort Whipple to fur-
nish you with military protection, and you
will call upon him at once, if in your judg-
ment it is necessary. On no account surrender United States property to Territorial
authorities. Keep Department notified."

"Oh, splendid!" cried Madge, clapping
her hands.

"Mr. Camp will find that other people
can give surprise parties as well as himself,"
I said cheerfully.

"You'll telegraph at once?" asked Mr.
Cullen.

"Instantly," I said, rising, and added,
"Don't you want to see what I say, Miss
Cullen?"

"Of course I do," she cried, jumping up
eagerly.

Lord Ralles scowled as he said, "Yes;
let's see what Mr. Superintendent has to
say."

"You need n't trouble yourself," I re-

marked, but he followed us into the station.
I was disgusted, but at the same time it
seemed to me that he had come because he
was jealous ; and that was n't an unpleasant
thought. Whatever his motive, he was a
third party in the writing of that telegram,
and had to stand by while Miss Cullen and
I discussed and draughted it. I did n't try to
make it any too brief, not merely asking for
a guard and when I might expect it, but giving as well a pretty full history of the case,
which was hardly necessary.

" You 'll bankrupt yourself," laughed
Madge. " You must let us pay."

" I 'll let you pay, Miss Cullen, if you
want," I offered. " How much is it, Welply ? " I asked, shoving the blanks in to the
operator.

" Nothin' for a lady," said Welply, grinning.

" There, Miss Cullen," I asked, " does
the East come up to that in gallantry ? "

" Do you really mean that there is no
charge ? " demanded Madge, incredulously,
with her purse in her hand.

"That's the size of it," said the operator.

"I'm not going to believe that!" cried Madge. "I know you are only deceiving me, and I really want to pay."

I laughed as I said, "Sometimes railroad superintendents can send messages free, Miss Cullen."

"How silly of me!" exclaimed Madge. Then she remarked, "How nice it is to be a railroad superintendent, Mr. Gordon! I should like to be one myself."

That speech really lifted me off my feet, but while I was thinking what response to make, I came down to earth with a bounce.

"Since the telegram's done," said Lord Ralles to Miss Cullen, in a cool, almost commanding tone, "suppose we take a walk."

"I don't think I care to this morning," answered Madge.

"I think you had better," insisted his lordship, with such a manner that I felt inclined to knock him down.

To my surprise, Madge seemed to hesitate,

and finally said, " I 'l' walk up and down the platform, if you wish '

Lord Ralles nodded, and they went out, leaving me in a state of mingled amazement and rage at the way he had cut me out. Try as I would, I was n't able to hit upon any theory that supplied a solution to the conduct of either Lord Ralles or Miss Cullen, unless they were engaged and Miss Cullen displeased him by her behavior to me. But Madge seemed such an honest, frank girl that I 'd have believed anything sooner than that she was only playing with me.

If I was perplexed, I was n't going to give Lord Ralles the right of way, and as soon as I had made certain that the telegram was safely started I joined the walkers. I don't think any of us enjoyed the hour that followed, but I did n't care how miserable I was myself, so long as I was certain that I was blocking Lord Ralles; and his grumpiness showed very clearly that my presence did that. As for Madge, I could n't make her out. I had always thought I understood women a little, but her conduct was beyond understanding.

Apparently Miss Cullen did n't altogether relish her position, for presently she said she was going to the car. "I'm sure you and Lord Ralles will be company enough for each other," she predicted, giving me a flash of her eyes which showed them full of suppressed merriment, even while her face was grave.

In spite of her prediction, the moment she was gone Lord Railes and I pulled apart about as quickly as a yard-engine can split a couple of cars.

I moped around for an hour, too unsettled mentally to do anything but smoke, and only waiting for an invitation or for some excuse to go into 218. About eleven o'clock I obtained the latter in another telegram, and went into the car at once.

"Telegram received," I read triumphantly " A detail of two companies of the Twelfth Cavalry, under the command of Captain Singer, is ordered to Ash Forks, and will start within an hour, arriving at five o'clock. C. D. OLMSTEAD, Adjutant.'"

"That won't do, Gordon," cried Mr. Cullen. "The mandamus will be here before that."

"Oh, don't say there is something more wrong!" sighed Madge.

"Won't it be safer to run while there is still time?" suggested Albert, anxiously.

"I was born lazy about running away," I said.

"Oh, but please, just for once," Madge begged. "We know already how brave you are."

I thought for a moment, not so much objecting, in truth, to the running away as to the running away from Madge.

"I'd do it for you," I said, looking at Miss Cullen so that she understood this time what I meant, without my using any emphasis, "but I don't see any need of making myself uncomfortable, when I can make the other side so. Come along and see if my method is n't quite as good."

We went to the station, and I told the operator to call Rock Butte; then I dictated ·

"Direct conductor of Phœnix No. 3 on its arrival at Rock Butte to hold it there till further orders. RICHARD GORDON. Superintendent."

"That will save my running and their chasing," I laughed; "though I'm afraid a long vait in Rock Butte won't improve their tempers."

The next few hours were pretty exciting ones to all of us, as can well be imagined. Most of the time was spent, I have to confess, in manœuvres and struggles between Lord Ralles and myself as to which should monopolize Madge, without either of us succeeding. I was so engrossed with the contest that I forgot all about the passage of time, and only when the sheriff strolled up to the station did I realize that the climax was at hand. As a joke I introduced him to the Cullens, and we all stood chatting til! far out on the hill to the south I saw a cloud of dust and quietly called Miss Cullen's attention to it. She and I went to 97 for my field-glasses, and the moment Madge looked through them she cried, —

" Yes, I can see horses, and, oh, there are the stars and stripes! I don't think I ever loved them so much before."

" I suppose we civilians will have to take a back seat now, Miss Cullen ? " I said ; and she answered me with a demure smile worth — well, I 'm not going to put a value on that smile.

" They 'll be here very quickly," she almost sang.

" You forget the clearness of the air," I said, and then asked the sheriff how far away the dust-cloud was.

" Yer mean that cattle-drive ? " he asked. " 'Bout ten miles."

" You seem to think of everything," exclaimed Miss Cullen, as if my knowing that distances are deceptive in Arizona was wonderful. I sometimes think one gets the most praise in this world for what least deserves it.

I waited half an hour to be safe, and then released No. 3, just as we were called to luncheon; and this time I did n't refuse the invitation to eat mine in 218.

We did n't hurry over the meal, and towards the end I took to looking at my watch, wondering what could keep the cavalry from arriving.

"I hope there is no danger of the train arriving first, is there?" asked Madge.

"Not the slightest," I assured her. "The train won't be here for an hour, and the cavalry had only five miles to cover forty minutes ago. I must say, they seem to be taking their time."

"There they are now!" cried Albert.

Listening, we heard the clatter of horses' feet, going at a good pace, and we all rose and went to the windows, to see the arrival. Our feelings can be judged when across the tracks came only a mob of thirty or forty cowboys, riding in their usual "show-off" style.

"The deuce!" I could n't help exclaiming, in my surprise. "Are you sure you saw a flag, Miss Cullen?"

"Why — I — thought — " she faltered. "I saw something red, and — I supposed of course — "

Not waiting to let her finish, I exclaimed, "There's been a fluke somewhere, I'm afraid; but we are still in good shape, for the train can't possibly be here under an hour. I'll get my field-glasses and have another look before I decide what — "

My speech was interrupted by the entrance of the sheriff and Mr. Camp!

CHAPTER XI

THE LETTERS CHANGE HANDS AGAIN

WHAT seemed at the moment an incompre-
hensible puzzle had, as we afterwards learned,
a very simple explanation. One of the G
S. directors, Mr. Baldwin, who had come in
on Mr. Camp's car, was the owner of a
great cattle-ranch near Rock Butte. When
the train had been held at that station for a
few minutes, Camp went to the conductor,
demanded the cause for the delay, and was
shown my telegram. Seeing through the
device, the party had at once gone to this
ranch, where the owner, Baldwin, mounted
them, and it was their dust-cloud we had
seen as they rode up to Ash Forks. To
make matters more serious, Baldwin had
rounded up his cowboys and brought them
along with him, in order to make any resistance impossible.

I made no objection to the sheriff serving the paper, though it nearly broke my heart to see Madge's face. To cheer her I said, suggestively, "They've got me, but they haven't got the letters, Miss Cullen. And, remember, it's always darkest before the dawn, and the stars in their courses are against Sisera."

With the sheriff and Mr. Camp I then walked over to the saloon, where Judge Wilson was waiting to dispose of my case. Mr. Cullen and Albert tried to come too, but all outsiders were excluded by order of the "court." I was told to show cause why I should not forthwith produce the letters, and answered that I asked an adjournment of the case so that I might be heard by counsel. It was denied, as was to have been expected; indeed, why they took the trouble to go through the forms was beyond me. I told Wilson I should not produce the letters, and he asked if I knew what that meant. I couldn't help laughing and retorting, —

"It very appropriately means 'contempt of the court,' your honor."

"I'll give you a stiff term, young man," he said.

"It will take just one day to have habeas corpus proceedings in a United States court, and one more to get the papers here," I rejoined pleasantly.

Seeing that I understood the moves too well to be bluffed, the judge, Mr. Camp, and the lawyer held a whispered consultation. My surprise can be imagined when, at its conclusion, Mr. Camp said,—

"Your honor, I charge Richard Gordon with being concerned in the holding up of the Missouri Western Overland No. 3 on the night of October 14, and ask that he be taken into custody on that charge."

I couldn't make out this new move, and puzzled over it, while Judge Wilson ordered my commitment. But the next step revealed the object, for the lawyer then asked for a search-warrant to look for stolen property.

The judge was equally obliging, and began to fill one out on the instant.

This made me feel pretty serious, for the letters were in my breast-pocket, and I swore at my own stupidity in not having put them in the station safe when I had first arrived at Ash Forks. There were n't many moments in which to think while the judge scribbled away at the warrant, but in what time there was I did a lot of head-work, without, however, finding more than one way out of the snarl. And when I saw the judge finish off his signature with a flourish, I played a pretty desperate card.

" You 're just too late, gentlemen," I said, pointing out the side window of the saloon. " There come the cavalry."

The three conspirators jumped to their feet and bolted for the window; even the sheriff turned to look. As he did so I gave him a shove towards the three which sent them all sprawling on the floor in a pretty badly mixed-up condition. I made a dash for the door, and as I went through it I grabbed the key and locked them in. When I turned to do so I saw the lot struggling up from the floor, and, knowing that it would n't take them many seconds to find their way out through the window, I did n't waste much time in watching them.

Camp, Baldwin, and the judge had left their horses just outside the saloon, and there they were still patiently standing, with their bridles thrown over their heads, as only Western horses will stand. It did n't take me long to have those bridles back in place, and as I tossed each over the peak of the Mexican saddle I gave two of the ponies slaps which started them off at a lope across the railroad tracks. I swung myself into the saddle of the third, and flicked him with the loose ends of the bridle in a way which made him understand that I meant business.

Baldwin's cowboys had most of them scattered to the various saloons of the place, but two of them were standing in the door-way of a store. I acted so quickly, however, that they did n't seem to take in what I was about till I was well mounted. Then I heard a yell, and fearing that they might shoot, — for the cowboy does love to use his gun, — I turned sharp at the saloon corner and rode up the side street, just in time to see Camp climbing through the window, with Baldwin's head in view behind him.

Before I had ridden a hundred feet I realized that I had a done-up horse under me, and, considering that he ha covered over forty miles that afternoon in pretty quick time, it was not surprising that there was n't very much go left in him. I knew that Baldwin's cowboys could get new mounts in plenty without wasting many minutes, and that then they would overhaul me in very short order. Clearly there was no use in my attempting to escape by running. And, as I was n't armed, my only hope was to beat them by some finesse.

Ash Forks, like all Western railroad towns, is one long line of buildings running parallel with the railway tracks. Two hundred feet, therefore, brought me to the edge of the town, and I wheeled my pony and rode down behind the rear of the buildings. In turning, I looked back, and saw half a dozen mounted men already in pursuit, but I lost sight of them the next moment. As soon as I reached a street leading back to the railroad I turned again, and rode towards it, my one thought being to get back, if possible, to the station, and put the letters into the railroad agent's safe.

When I reached the main street I saw that my hope was futile, for another batch of cowboys were coming in full gallop towards me, very thoroughly heading me off in that direction. To escape them, I headed up the street away from the station, with the pack in close pursuit. They yelled at me to hold up, and I expected every moment to hear the crack of revolvers, for the poorest shot among them would have found no difficulty in dropping my horse at that distance if they had wanted to stop me. It isn't a very nice sensation to keep your ears pricked up in expectation of hearing the shooting begin, and to know that any moment may be your last. I don't suppose I was on the ragged edge more than thirty seconds, but they were enough to prove to me that to keep one's back turned to an enemy as one runs away takes a deal more pluck than to stand up and face his gun. Fortunately for me, my pursuers felt so sure of my capture that not one of them drew a bead on me.

The moment I saw that there was no escape, I put my hand in my breast-pocket and took out the letters, intending to tear them into a hundred pieces. But as I did so I realized that to destroy United States mail not merely entailed criminal liability, but was off color morally. I faltered, balancing the outwitting of Camp against State's prison, the doing my best for Madge against the wrong of it. I think I'm as honest a fellow as the average, but I have to confess that I could n't decide to do right till I thought that Madge would n't want me to be dishonest, even for her.

I turned across the railroad tracks, and cut in behind some freight-cars that were standing on a siding. This put me out of view of my pursuers for a moment, and in that instant I stood up in my stirrups, lifted the broad leather flap of the saddle, and tucked the letters underneath it, as far in as I could force them. It was a desperate place in which to hide them, but the game was a desperate one at best, and the very boldness of the idea might be its best chance of success.

I was now heading for the station over the ties, and was surprised to see Fred Cullen with Lord Ralles on the tracks up by the special, for my mind had been so busy in the last hour that I had forgotten that Fred was due. The moment I saw him, I rode towards him, pressing my pony for all he was worth. My hope was that I might get time to give Fred the tip as to where the letters were; but before I was within speaking distance Baldwin came running out from behind the station, and, seeing me, turned, called back and gesticulated, evidently to summon some cowboys to head me off.

Afraid to shout anything which should convey the slightest clue as to the whereabouts of the letters, as the next best thing I pulled a couple of old section reports from my pocket, intending to ride up and run into my car, for I knew that the papers in my hand would be taken to be the wanted letters, and that if I could only get inside the car even for a moment the suspicion would be that I had been able to hide them. Unfortunately, the plan was no sooner thought of than I heard the whistle of a lariat, and before I could guard myself the noose settled over my head. I threw the papers towards Fred and Lord Ralles, shouting, "Hide them!" Fred was quick as a flash, and, grabbing them off the ground, sprang up the steps of my car and ran inside, just escaping a bullet from my pursuers. I tried to pull up my pony, for I did not want to be jerked off, but I was too late, and the next moment I was lying on the ground in a pretty well shaken and jarred condition, surrounded by a lot of men.

CHAPTER XII

AN EVENING IN JAIL

BEFORE my ideas had had time to straighten themselves out, I was lifted to my feet, and half pushed, half lifted to the station platform. Camp was already there, and as I took this fact in I saw Frederic and his lordship pulled through the doorway of my car by the cowboys and dragged out on the platform beside me. The reports were now in Lord Ralles's hands.

"That's what we want, boys," cried Camp. "Those letters."

"Take your hands off me," said Lord Ralles, coolly, "and I'll give them to you."

The men who had hold of his arms let go of him, and quick as a flash Ralles tore the papers in two. He tried to tear them once more, but, before he could do so, half a dozen men were holding him, and the papers were forced out of his hands.

Albert Cullen — for all of them were on the platform of 218 by this time — shouted, " Well done, Ralles ! " quite forgetting in the excitement of the moment his English accent and drawl.

Apparently Camp did n't agree with him, for he ripped out a string of oaths which he impartially divided among Ralles, the cowboys, and myself. I was decidedly sorry that I had n't given the real letters, for his lordship clearly had no scruple about destroying them, and I knew few men whom I would have seen behind prison-bars with as little personal regret. However, no one had, so far as I could see, paid the slightest attention to the pony, and the probabilities were that he was already headed for Baldwin's ranch, with no likelihood of his stopping till he reached home. At least that was what I hoped ; but there were a lot of ponies standing about, and, not knowing the markings of the one I had ridden, I was n't able to tell whether he might not be among them.

Just as the fragments of the papers were passed over to Mr. Camp, he was joined by Baldwin and the judge, and Camp held the torn pieces up to them, saying, —

" They 've torn the proxies in two."

" Don't let that trouble you," said the judge. " Make an affidavit before me, reciting the manner in which they were destroyed, and I 'll grant you a mandamus compelling the directors to accept them as bona-fide proxies. Let me see how much injured they are."

Camp unfolded the papers, and I chuckled to myself at the look of surprise that over-spread his face as he took in the fact that they were nothing but section reports. And, though I don't like cuss-words, I have to acknowledge that I enjoyed the two or three that he promptly ejaculated.

When the first surprise of the trio was over, they called on the sheriff, who arrived opportunely, to take us into 97 and search the three of us, — a proceeding that puzzled Fred and his lordship not a little, for they were n't on to the fact that the letters had n't been recovered. I presume the latter will some day write a book dwelling on the favorite theme of the foreigner, that there is no personal privacy in America, and I don't know but his experiences justify the view. The running remarks as the search was made seemed to open Fred's eyes, for he looked at me with a puzzled air, but I winked and frowned at him, and he put his face in order.

When the papers were not found on any of us, Camp and Baldwin both nearly went demented. Baldwin suggested that I had never had the papers, but Camp argued that Fred or Lord Ralles must have hidden them in the car, in spite of the fact that the cowboys who had caught them insisted that they could n't have had time to hide the papers. Anyway, they spent an hour in ferreting about in my car, and even searched my two darkies, on the possibility that the true letters had been passed on to them.

While they were engaged in this, I was trying to think out some way of letting Mr. Cullen and Albert know where the letters were. The problem was to suggest the saddle to them, without letting the cowboys understand, and by good luck I thought I had the means. Albert had complained to me the day we had ridden out to the Indian dwellings at Flagstaff that his saddle fretted some galled spots which he had chafed on his trip to Moran's Point. Hoping he would "catch on," I shouted to him, —

"How are your sore spots, Albert?"

He looked at me in a puzzled way, and called, "Aw, I don't understand you."

"Those sore spots you complained about to me the day before yesterday," I explained.

He did n't seem any the less befogged as he replied, "I had forgotten all about them."

"I've got a touch of the same trouble,"

I went on; "and, if I were you, I'd look into the cause."

Albert only looked very much mystified, and I did n't dare say more, for at this point the trio, with the sheriff, came out of my car. If I had n't known that the letters were safe, I could have read the story in their faces, for more disgusted and angry-looking men I have rarely seen.

They had a talk with the sheriff, and then Fred, Lord Ralles, and I were marched off by the official, his lordship loudly demanding sight of a warrant, and protesting against the illegality of his arrest, varied at moments by threats to appeal to the British consul, minister plenipo., her Majesty's Foreign Office, etc., all of which had about as much influence on the sheriff and his cowboy assistants as a Moqui Indian snake-dance would have in stopping a runaway engine. I confess to feeling a certain grim satisfaction in the fact that if I was to be shut off from seeing Madge, the Britisher was in the same box with me.

Ash Forks, though only six years old, had advanced far enough towards civilization to have a small jail, and into that we were shoved. Night was come by the time we were lodged there, and, being in pretty good appetite, I struck the sheriff for some grub.

"I'll git yer somethin'," he said, good-naturedly; "but next time yer shove people, Mr. Gordon, just quit shovin' yer friends. My shoulder feels like — " perhaps it's just as well not to say what his shoulder felt like. The Western vocabulary is expressive, but at times not quite fit for publication.

The moment the sheriff was gone, Fred wanted the mystery of the letters explained, and I told him all there was to tell, including as good a description of the pony as I could give him. We tried to hit on some plan to get word to those outside, but it was n't to be done. At least it was a point gained that some one of our party besides myself knew where the letters were.

The sheriff returned presently with a loaf

of canned bread and a tin of beans. If I
had been alone, I should have kicked at the
food and got permission for my darkies to
send me up something from 97; but I
thought I'd see how Lord Ralles would
like genuine Western fare, so I said nothing. That, I have to state, is more — or
rather less — than the Britisher did, after
he had sampled the stuff; and really I don't
blame him, much as I enjoyed his rage and
disgust.

It did n't take long to finish our supper,
and then Fred, who had n't slept much the
night before, stretched out on the floor and
went to sleep. Lord Ralles and I sat on
boxes — the only furniture the room con-
tained — about as far apart as we could get,
he in the sulks, and I whistling cheerfully.
I should have liked to be with Madge, but
he was n't; so there was some compensation, and I knew that time was playing the
cards in our favor: so long as they had n't
found the letters we had only to sit still to
win.

About an hour after supper, the sheriff came back and told me Camp and Baldwin wanted to see me. I saw no reason to object, so in they came, accompanied by the judge. Baldwin opened the ball by saying genially, —

" Well, Mr. Gordon, you 've played a pretty cute gamble, and I suppose you think you stand to win the pot."

" I 'm not complaining," I said.

" Still," snarled Camp, angrily, as if my contented manner fretted him, " our time will come presently, and we can make it pretty uncomfortable for you. Illegal proceedings put a man in jail in the long run."

" I hope you take your lesson to heart," I remarked cheerfully, which made Camp scowl worse than ever.

" Now," said Baldwin, who kept cool, " we know you are not risking loss of position and the State's prison for nothing, and we want to know what there is in it for you ? "

"I would n't stake my chance of State's prison against yours, gentlemen. And, while I may lose my position, I 'll be a long way from starvation."

"That does n't tell us what Cullen gives you to take the risk."

"Mr. Cullen has n't given, or even hinted that he 'll give, anything."

"And Mr. Gordon has n't asked, and, if I know him, would n't take a cent for what he has done," said Fred, rising from the floor.

"You mean to say you are doing it for nothing?" exclaimed Camp, incredulously.

"That 's about the truth of it," I said; though I thought of Madge as I said it, and felt guilty in suggesting that she was nothing.

"Then what is your motive?" cried Baldwin.

If there had been any use, I should have replied, "The right;" but I knew that they would only think I was posing if I said it. Instead I replied: "Mr. Cullen's party has the stock majority in their favor, and would have won a fair fight if you had played fair. Since you did n't, I 'm doing my best to put things to rights."

Camp cried, " All the more fool — " but Baldwin interrupted him by saying, —

" That only shows what a mean cuss Cullen is. He ought to give you ten thousand, if he gives you a cent."

" Yes," cried Camp, " those letters are worth money, whether he 's offered it or not."

" Mr. Cullen never so much as hinted paying me," said I.

" Well, Mr. Gordon," said Baldwin, suavely, " we 'll show you that we can be more liberal. Though the letters rightfully belong to Mr. Camp, if you 'll deliver them to us we 'll see that you don't lose your place, and we 'll give you five thousand dollars."

I glanced at Fred, whom I found looking at me anxiously, and asked him, —

" Can't you do better than that ? "

"We could with any one but you," said Fred.

I should have liked to shake hands over this compliment, but I only nodded, and turning to Mr. Camp, said, —

"You see how mean they are."

"You'll find we are not built that way," said Baldwin. "Five thousand is n't a bad day's work, eh?"

"No," I said, laughing; "but you just told me I ought to get ten thousand if I got a cent."

"It's worth ten to Mr. Cullen, but —"

I interrupted by saying, "If it's worth ten to him, it's worth a hundred to me."

That was too much for Camp. First he said something best omitted, and then went on, "I told you it was waste time trying to win him over."

The three stood apart for a moment whispering, and then Judge Wilson called the sheriff over, and they all went out together. The moment we were alone, Frederic held out his hand, and said, —

"Gordon, it's no use saying anything, but if we can ever do — "

I merely shook hands, but I wanted the worst way to say, —

"Tell Madge what I've done, and the thing's square."

CHAPTER XIII

A LESSON IN POLITENESS

WITHIN five minutes we had a big surprise, for the sheriff and Mr. Baldwin came back, and the former announced that Fred and Lord Ralles were free, having been released on bail. When we found that Baldwin had gone on the bond, I knew that there was a scheme of some sort in the move, and, taking Fred aside, I warned him against trying to recover the proxies.

"They probably think that one or the other of you knows where the letters are hidden," I whispered, "and they'll keep a watch on you; so go slow."

He nodded, and followed the sheriff and Lord Ralles out.

The moment they were gone, Mr. Camp said, "I came back to give you a last chance."

"That's very good of you," I said.

"I warn you," he muttered threateningly, "we are not men to be beaten. There are fifty cowboys of Baldwin's in this town, who think you were concerned in the holding up. By merely tipping them the wink, they'll have you out of this, and after they've got you outside I wouldn't give the toss of a nickel for your life. Now, then, will you hand over those letters, or will you go to —— inside of ten minutes?"

I lost my temper in turn. "I'd much prefer going to some place where I was less sure of meeting you," I retorted; "and as for the cowboys, you'll have to be as tricky with them as you want to be with me before you'll get them to back you up in your dirty work."

At this point the sheriff called back to ask Camp if he was coming.

"All right," cried Camp, and went to the door. "This is the last call," he snarled, pausing for a moment on the threshold.

"I hope so," said I, more calmly in

manner than in feeling, I have to acknowledge, for I did n't like the look of things. That they were in earnest I felt pretty certain, for I understood now why they had let my companions out of jail. They knew that angry cowboys were a trifle undiscriminating, and did n't care to risk hanging more than was necessary.

A long time seemed to pass after they were gone, but in reality it was n't more than fifteen minutes before I heard some one steal up and softly unlock the door. I confess the evident endeavor to do it quietly gave me a scare, for it seemed to me it could n't be an above-board movement. Thinking this, I picked up the box on which I had been sitting and prepared to make the best fight I could. It was a good deal of relief, therefore, when the door opened just wide enough for a man to put in his head, and I heard the sheriff's voice say, softly, —

" Hi, Gordon ! "

I was at the door in an instant, and asked, —

" What 's up ? "

" They 're gettin' the fellers together, and sayin' that yer shot a woman in the hold-up."

" It 's an infernal lie," I said.

"Sounds that way to me," assented the sheriff; " but two-thirds of the boys are drunk, and it 's a long time since they 've had any fun."

" Well," I said, as calmly as I could, " are you going to stand by me ? "

" I would, Mr. Gordon," he replied, " if there was any good, but there ain't time to get a posse, and what 's one Winchester against a mob of cowboys like them ? "

" If you 'll lend me your gun," I said, " I 'll show just what it is worth, without troubling you."

" I 'll do better than that," offered the sheriff, " and that 's what I 'm here for. Just sneak, while there 's time."

" You mean —? " I exclaimed.

" That 's it. I 'm goin' away, and I 'll leave the door unlocked. If yer get clear let me know yer address, and later, if I want yer, I'll send yer word." He took a grip on my fingers that numbed them as if they had been caught in an air-brake, and disappeared.

I slipped out after the sheriff without loss of time. That there was n't much to spare was shown by a crowd with some torches down the street, collected in front of a saloon. They were making a good deal of noise, even for the West; evidently the flame was being fanned. Not wasting time, I struck for the railroad, because I knew the geography of that best, but still more because I wanted to get to the station. It was a big risk to go there, but it was one I was willing to take for the object I had in view, and, since I had to take it, it was safest to get through with the job before the discovery was made that I was no longer in jail.

It did n't take me three minutes to reach the station. The whole place was black as a coal-dumper, except for the slices of light which shone through the cracks of the curtained windows in the specials, the dim light of the lamp in the station, and the glow of

the row of saloons two hundred feet away.
I was afraid, however, that there might be a
spy lurking somewhere, for it was likely that
Camp would hope to get some clue of the
letters by keeping a watch on the station
and the cars. Thinking boldness the safest
course, I walked on to the platform without
hesitation, and went into the station. The
" night man " was sitting in his chair, nodding, but he waked up the moment I
spoke.

"Don't speak my name," I said, warn-
ingly, as he struggled to his feet; and then in
the fewest possible words I told him what I
wanted of him, — to find if the pony I had
ridden (Camp's or Baldwin's) was in town
and, if so, to learn where it was, and to get
the letters on the quiet from under the
saddle-flap. I chose this man, first, because
I could trust him, and next, because I had
only one of the Cullens as an alternative,
and if any of them went sneaking round, it
would be sure to attract attention. " The
moment you have the letters, put them in

the station safe," I ended, "and then get word to me."

"And where'll you be, Mr. Gordon?" asked the man.

"Is there any place about here that's a safe hiding spot for a few hours?" I asked. "I want to stay till I'm sure those letters are safe, and after that I'll steal on board the first train that comes along."

"Then you'll want to be near here," said the man. "I'll tell you, I've got just the place for you. The platform's boarded in all round, but I noticed one plank that's loose at one end, right at this nigh corner, and if you just pry it open enough to get in, and then pull the board in place, they'll never find you."

"That will do," I said; "and when the letters are safe, come out on the platform, walk up and down once, bang the door twice, and then say, 'That way freight is late.' And if you get a chance, tell one of the Cullens where I'm hidden."

I crossed the platform boldly, jumped

down, and walked away. But after going
fifty feet I dropped down on my hands and
knees and crawled back. Inside of two
minutes I was safely stowed away under the
platform, in about as neat a hiding-place as a
man could ask. In fact, if I had only had
my wits enough about me to borrow a revolver of the man, I could have made a
pretty good defence, even if discovered.

Underneath the platform was loose gravel,
and, as an additional precaution, I scooped
out, close to the side-boarding, a trough long
enough for me to lie in. Then I got into
the hole, shovelled the sand over my legs,
and piled the rest up in a heap close to me,
so that by a few sweeps of my arm I could
cover my whole body, leaving only my
mouth and nose exposed, and those below
the level. That made me feel pretty safe,
for, even if the cowboys found the loose
plank and crawled in, it would take un-
common good eyesight, in the darkness, to
find me. I had hollowed out my living
grave to fit, and if I could have smoked, I

should have been decidedly comfortable.
Sleep I dared not indulge in, and the sequel
showed that I was right in not allowing myself that luxury.

I had n't much more than comfortably
settled myself, and let thoughts of a cigar
and a nap flit through my mind, when a row
up the street showed that the jail-breaking
had been discovered. Then followed shouts
and confusion for a few moments, while a
search was being organized. I heard some
horsemen ride over the tracks, and also down
the street, followed by the hurried footsteps
of half a dozen men. Some banged at the
doors of the specials, while others knocked at
the station door.

One of the Cullers servants opened
the door of 218, and I heard the sheriff's
voice telling him he 'd got to search the
car. The darky protested, saying that the
" gentmun was all away, and only de miss
inside." The row brought Miss Cullen to
the door, and I heard her ask what was the
matter.

"Sorry to trouble yer, miss," said the sheriff, "but a prisoner has broken jail, and we 've got to look for him."

"Escaped ! " cried Madge, joyfully. "How ? "

"That 's just what gits away with me," marvelled the sheriff. "My idee is — "

"Don't waste time on theories," said Camp's voice, angrily. "Search the car."

"Sorry to discommode a lady," apologized the sheriff, gallantly, "but if we may just look around a little ? "

"My father and brothers went out a few minutes ago," said Madge, hesitatingly, "and I don't know if they would be willing."

Camp laughed angrily, and ordered, "Stand aside, there."

"Don't yer worry," said the sheriff "If he 's on the car, he can't git away. We 'll send a feller up for Mr. Cullen, while we search Mr. Gordon's car and the station."

They set about it at once, and used up ten

minutes in the task. Then I heard Camp say, —

"Come, we can't wait all night for permission to search this car. Go ahead."

"I hope you'll wait till my father comes," begged Madge.

"Now go slow, Mr. Camp," said the sheriff. "We must n't discomfort the lady if we can avoid it."

"I believe you're wasting time in order to help him escape," snapped Camp.

"Nothin' of the kind," denied the sheriff.

"If you won't do your duty, I'll take the law into my own hands, and order the car searched," sputtered Camp, so angry as hardly to be able to articulate.

"Look a here," growled the sheriff, "who are yer sayin' all this to anyway? If yer talkin' to me, say so right off."

"All I mean," hastily said Camp, "is that it's your duty, in your honorable position, to search this car."

"I don't need no instructin' in my dooty as sheriff," retorted the official. "But a bigger dooty is what is owin' to the feminine sex. When a female is in question, a gentleman, Mr. Camp, — yes, sir, a gentleman, — is in dooty bound to be perlite."

" Politeness be —— —— ! " swore Camp.

" Git as angry as yer —— please," roared the sheriff wrathfully, " but —— my soul to —— if any —————— cuss has a right to use such —— —— talk in the presence of a lady ! "

CHAPTER XIV

" LISTENERS NEVER HEAR ANYTHING GOOD "

BEFORE I had ceased chuckling over the sheriff's indignant declaration of the canons of etiquette, I heard Mr. Cullen's voice demanding to know what the trouble was, and it was quickly explained to him that I had escaped. He at once gave them permission to search his car, and went in with the sheriff and the cowboys. Apparently Madge went in too, for in a moment I heard Camp say, in a low voice, —

" Two of you fellows get down below the car and crawl in under the truck where you can't be seen. Evidently that cuss is n't here, but he 's likely to come by and by. If so, nab him if you can, and if you can't, fire two shots. Mosely, are you heeled ? "

" Do I chaw terbaccy ? " asked Mosely,

ironically, clearly insulted at the suggestion that he would travel without a gun.

" Then keep a sharp lookout, and listen to everything you hear, especially the where-abouts of some letters. If you can spot their lay, crawl out and get word to me at once. Now, under you go before they come out."

I heard two men drop into the gravel close alongside of where I lay, and then crawl under the truck of 218. They were n't a moment too soon, for the next instant I heard two or three people jump on to the platform, and Albert Cullen's voice drawl, " Aw, by Jove, what's the row ? " Camp not enlightening them, Lord Ralles suggested that they get on the car to find out, and the three did so. A moment later the sheriff came to the door and told Camp that I was not to be found.

" I told yer this was the last place to look for the cuss, Mr. Camp," he said. " We 've just discomforted the lady for nothin'."

" Then we must search elsewhere," spoke up Camp. " Come on, boys."

The sheriff turned and made another elaborate apology for having had to trouble the lady.

I heard Madge tell him that he had n't troubled her at all, and then, as the cowboys and Camp walked off, she added, " And, Mr. Gunton, I want to thank you for reproving Mr. Camp's dreadful swearing."

" Thank yer, miss," said the sheriff. " We fellers are a little rough at times, but —— me if we don't know what 's due to a lady."

" Papa," said Madge, as soon as he was out of hearing, " the sheriff is the most beautiful swearer I ever heard."

For a while there was silence round the station; I suppose the party in 218 were comparing notes, while the two cowboys and I had the best reasons for being quiet. Presently, however, the men came out of the car and jumped down on the platform. Madge evidently followed them to the door, for she called, " Please let me know the moment something happens or you learn anything."

"Better go to bed, Madgy," Albert called. "You'll only worry, and it's after three."

"I couldn't sleep if I tried," she answered.

Their footsteps died away in a moment, and I heard her close the door of 218. In a few moments she opened it again, and, stepping down to the station platform, began to pace up and down it. If I had only dared, I could have put my finger through the crack of the planks and touched her foot as she walked over my head, but I was afraid it might startle her into a shriek, and there was no explaining to her what it meant without telling the cowboys how close they were to their quarry.

Madge hadn't walked from one end of the platform to the other more than three or four times, when I heard some one coming. She evidently heard it also, for she said, —

"I began to be afraid you hadn't understood me."

"I thought you told me to see first if I were needed," responded a voice that even the distance and the planks did not prevent me from recognizing as that of Lord Ralles.

"Yes," said she. "You are sure you can be spared?"

"I could n't be of the slightest use," asserted Ralles, getting on to the platform and joining Madge. "It's as black as ink everywhere, and I don't think there's anything to be done till daylight."

"Then I'm glad you came back, for I really want to say something,—to ask the greatest favor of you."

"You only have to tell me what it is," said his lordship.

"Even that is very hard," murmured Madge. "If—if— Oh! I'm afraid I have n't the courage, after all."

"I'll be glad to do anything I can."

"It's—well— Oh, dear, I can't. Let's walk a little, while I think how to put it."

They began to walk, which took a weight off my mind, as I had been forced to hear every word thus far spoken, and was dread-

ing what might follow, since I was perfectly
helpless to warn them. The platform was
built around the station, and in a moment
they were out of hearing.

Before many seconds were over, however,
they had walked round the building, and I
heard Lord Ralles say, —

" You really don't mean that he 's insulted
you ? "

" That is just what I do mean," cried
Madge, indignantly. " It 's been almost past
endurance. I have n't dared to tell any one,
but he had the cruelty, the meanness, on
Hance's trail to threaten that — "

At that point the walkers turned the corner
again, and I could not hear the rest of the
sentence. But I had heard more than enough
to make me grow hot with mortification,
even while I could hardly believe I had understood aright. Madge had been so kind to
me lately that I could n't think she had been
feeling as bitterly as she spoke. That such
an apparently frank girl was a consummate
actress was n't to be thought, and yet — I

remembered how well she had played her part
on Hance's trail; but even that would n't
convince me. Proof of her duplicity came
quickly enough, for, while I was still thinking, the walkers were round again, and Lord
Ralles was saying, —

" Why have n't you complained to your
father or brothers ? "

" Because I knew they would resent his
conduct to me, and — "

" Of course they would," cried her companion, interrupting. " But why should you
object to that ? "

" Because of the letters," explained Madge.
" Don't you see that if we made him angry
he would betray us to Mr. Camp, and — "

Then they passed out of hearing, leaving
me almost desperate, both at being an eaves-
dropper to such a conversation, and that
Madge could think so meanly of me. To
say it, too, to Lord Ralles made it cut all
the deeper, as any fellow who has been in
love will understand.

Round they came again in a moment, and

I braced myself for the lash of the whip that I felt was coming. I didn't escape it, for Madge was saying, —

"Can you conceive of a man pretending to care for a girl and yet treating her so? I can't tell you the grief, the mortification, I have endured." She spoke with a half-sob in her throat, as if she was struggling not to cry, which made me wish I had never been born. "It's been all I could do to control myself in his presence, I have come so utterly to hate and despise him," she added.

"I don't wonder," growled Lord Ralles. "My only surprise is — "

With that they passed out of hearing again, leaving me fairly desperate with shame, grief, and, I'm afraid, with anger. I felt at once guilty and yet wronged. I knew my conduct on the trail must have seemed to her ungentlemanly because I had never dared to explain that my action there had been a pure bluff, and that I wouldn't have really searched her for — well, for anything; but though she might think badly of me for that, yet I had done my best to counterbalance it, and was running big risks, both present and eventual, for Madge's sake. Yet here she was acknowledging that thus far she had used me as a puppet, while all the time disliking me. It was a terrible blow, made all the harder by the fact that she was proving herself such a different girl from the one I loved, — so different, in fact, that, despite what I had heard, I could n't quite believe it of her, and found myself seeking to extenuate and even justify her conduct. While I was doing this, they came within hearing, and Lord Ralles was speaking.

" — with you," he said. " But I still do not see what I can do, however much I may wish to serve you."

" Can't you go to him and insist that he — or tell him what I really feel towards him — or anything, in fact, to shame him ? I really can't go on acting longer."

That reached the limit of my endurance, and I crawled from my burrow, intending to get out from under that platform, whether I was caught or not. I know it was a foolish move; after having heard what I had, a little more or less was quite immaterial. But I entirely forgot my danger, in the sting of what Madge had said, and my one thought was to stand face to face with her long enough to — I'm sure I don't know what I intended to say.

Just as 1 reached the plank, however, I heard Lord Ralles ask, —

" Who's that ? "

" It's me," said a voice, — " the station agent." Then I heard a door close. Some one walked out to the centre of the platform and remarked, —

" That 'ere way freight is late."

At least the letters were recovered.

CHAPTER XV

THE SURRENDER OF THE LETTERS

IF the letters were safe, that was a good deal more than I was. The moment the station-master had made his agreed-upon announcement, he said to the walkers, —

" Had any news of Mr. Gordon ? "

" No," replied Lord Ralles. " And, as the lights keep moving in the town, they must still be hunting for him."

" I reckon they 'll do considerable more huntin' before they find him up there," chuckled the man, with a self-important manner. " He 's hidden away under this ere platform."

" Not right here ? " I heard Madge cry, but I had too much to do to take in what followed. I was lying close to the loose plank, and even before the station-master had completed his sentence I was squirming through the crack. As I freed my legs I heard two shots, which I knew was the signal given by the cowboys, followed by a shriek of fright from Madge, for which she was hardly to be blamed. I was on my feet in an instant and ran down the tracks at my best speed. It was n't with much hope of escape, for once out from under the planking I found, what I had not before realized, that day was dawning, and already outlines at a distance could be seen. However, I was bound to do my best, and I did it.

Before I had run a hundred feet I could hear pursuers, and a moment later a revolver cracked, ploughing up the dust in front of me. Another bullet followed, and, seeing that affairs were getting desperate, I dodged round the end of some cars, only to plump into a man running at full speed. The collision was so unexpected that we both fell, and before I could get on my feet one of my pursuers plumped down on top of me and I felt something cold on the back of my neck.

" Lie still, yer sneakin' coyote of a road agent," said the man, " or I 'll blow yer so full of lead that yer could n't float in Salt Lake."

I preferred to 'ake his advice, and lay quiet while the cowboys gathered. From all directions I heard them coming, calling to each other that " the skunk that shot the woman is corralled," and other forms of the same information. In a moment I was jerked to my feet, only to be swept off them with equal celerity, and was half carried, half dragged, along the tracks. It was n't as rough handling as I have taken on the foot-ball-field, but I did n't enjoy it.

In a space of time that seemed only seconds, I was close to a telegraph-pole; but, brief as the moment had been, a fellow with a lariat tied round his waist was half-way up the post. I knew the mob had been told that I had killed a woman in the hold-up, for the cowboy, bad as he is, has his own standards, beyond which he won't go. But I might as well have tried to tell my innocence to the moon as to get them to listen to denials, even if I could have made my voice heard.

The lariat was dropped over the cross-piece, and as a man adjusted the noose a sudden silence fell. 1 thought it was a little sense of what they were doing, but it was merely due to the command of Baldwin, who, with Camp, stood just outside the mob.

" Let me say a word before you pull," he called, and then to me he said, " Now will you give up the property ? "

I was pretty pale and shaky, but I come of stiffish stock, and I.would n't have backed down then, it seemed to me, if they had been going to boil me alive. I suppose it sounds foolish, and if I had had plenty of time I have no doubt my common-sense would have made me crawl. Not having time, I was on the point of saying " No," when the door of 218, which lay about two hundred yards away, flew open, and out came Mr. Cullen, Fred, Albert, Lord Ralles, and Captain Ackland, all with rifles. Of course it was perfect desperation for the five to tackle the cowboys, but they were game to do it, all the same.

How it would have ended I don't know, but as they sprang off the car platform Miss Cullen came out on it, and stood there, one hand holding on to the door-way, as if she needed support, and the other covering her heart. It was too far for me to see her face, but the whole attitude expressed such suffering that it was terrible to see. What was more, her position put her in range of every shot the cowboys might fire at the five as they charged. If I could have stopped them I would have done so, but, since that was impossible, I cried, —

" Mr. Camp, I 'll surrender the letters."

" Hold on, boys," shouted Baldwin; " wait till we get the property he stole." And, coming through the crowd, he threw the noose off my neck.

" Don't shoot, Mr. Cullen," I yelled, as my friends halted and raised their rifles, and, fortunately, the cowboys had opened up enough to let them hear me and see that I was free of the rope.

Escorted by Camp, Baldwin, and the cowboys, I walked towards them. On the way Baldwin said, in a low voice, " Deliver the letters, and we 'll tell the boys there has been a mistake. Otherwise — "

When we came up to the five, I called to them that I had agreed to surrender the letters. While I was saying it, Miss Cullen joined them, and it was curious to see how respectfully the cowboys took off their hats and fell back.

" You are quite right," Mr. Cullen called. " Give them the letters at once."

" Oh, do, Mr. Gordon," said Madge, still white and breathless with emotion. " The money is nothing. Don't think — " It was all she could say.

I felt pretty small, but with Camp and Baldwin, now reinforced by Judge Wilson, I went to the station, ordered the agent to open the safe, took out the three letters, and handed them to Mr. Camp, realizing how

poor Madge must have felt on Hance's trail.
It was a pretty big take down to my pride
I tell you, and made all the worse by the
way the three gloated over the letters and
over our defeat.

"We've taught you a lesson, young
man," sneered Camp, as after opening the
envelopes, to assure himself that the proxies
were all right, he tucked them into his
pocket. "And we'll teach you another one
after to-day's election."

Just as he concluded, we heard outside the
first note of a bugle, and as it sounded "By
fours, column left," my heart gave a big jump,
and the blood came rushing to my face.
Camp, Baldwin, and Wilson broke for the
door, but I got there first, and prevented their
escape. They tried to force their way through,
but I had n't blocked and interfered at football for nothing, and they might as well have
tried to break through the Sierras. Discov-
ing this, Camp whipped out his gun, and
told me to let them out. Being used to the
West, I recognized the goodness of the argu-

ment and stepped out on the platform, giving them free passage. But the twenty seconds I had delayed them had cooked their goose, for outside was a squadron of cavalry swinging a circle round the station; and we had barely reached the platform when the bugle sounded " Halt," quickly followed by " Forward left." As the ranks wheeled, and closed up as a solid line about us, I could have cheered with delight. There was a moment's dramatic hush, in which we could all hear the breathing of the winded horses, and then came the clatter of sword and spurs, as an officer sprang from his saddle.

" I want Richard Gordon," the officer called.

I responded, " At your service, and badly in need of yours, Captain Singer."

" Hope the delay has n't spoilt things," said the captain. " We had a cursed fool of a guide, who took the wrong trail and ran us into Limestone Cañon, where we had to camp for the night."

I explained the situation as quickly as I

could, and the captain's eyes gleamed. "I'd have given a bad quarter to have got here ten minutes sooner and ridden my men over those scoundrels," he muttered. "I saw them scatter as we rode up, and if I'd known what they'd been doing we'd have given them a volley." Then he walked over to Mr. Camp and said, "Give me those letters."

"I hold those letters by virtue of an order —" Camp began.

"Give me those letters," the captain interrupted.

"Do you intend a high-handed interference with the civil authorities?" Judge Wilson demanded.

"Come, come," said the captain, sternly. "You have taken forcible possession of United States property. Any talk about civil authorities is rubbish, and you know it."

"I will never —" cried Mr. Camp.

"Corporal Jackson, dismount a guard of six men," rang the captain's voice, interrupting him.

Evidently something in the voice or order convinced Mr. Camp, for the letters were hastily produced and given to Singer, who at once handed them to me. I turned with them to the Cullens, and, laughing, quoted, "'All's well that ends well.'"

But they did n't seem to care a bit about the recovery of the letters, and only wanted to have a hand-shake all round over my escape. Even Lord Ralles said, " Glad we could be of a little service," and did n't refuse my thanks, though the deuce knows they were badly enough expressed, in my consciousness that I had done an ungentle-manly trick over those trousers of his, and that he had been above remembering it when I was in real danger. I 'm ashamed enough to confess that when Miss Cullen held out her hand I made believe not to see it. I 'm a bad hand at pretending, and I saw Madge color up at my act.

The captain finally called me off to consult about our proceedings. I felt no very strong love for Camp, Baldwin, or Wilson, but I did n't see that a military arrest would accomplish anything, and after a little discussion it was decided to let them alone, as we could well afford to do, having won.

This matter decided, I said to the captain, " I 'll be obliged if you 'll put a guard round my car. And then, if you and your officers will come inside it, I have a — something in a bottle, recommended for removing alkali dust from the tonsils."

" Very happy to test your prescription," responded Singer, genially.

I started to go with him, but I could n't resist turning to Mr. Camp and his friends and saying, —

" Gentlemen, the G. S. is a big affair, but it is n't quite big enough to fight the U. S."

CHAPTER XVI

A GLOOMY GOOD-BY

AT that point my importance ceased. Apparently seeing that the game was up, Mr. Camp later in the morning asked Mr. Cullen to give him an interview, and when he was allowed to pass the sentry he came to the steps and suggested, —

'" Perhaps we can arrange a compromise between the Missouri Western and the Great Southern ? "

" We can try," Mr. Cullen assented. " Come into my car." He made way for Mr. Camp, and was about to follow him, when Madge took hold of her father's arm, and, making him stoop, whispered something to him.

" What kind ef a place ? " asked Mr Cullen, laughing.

" A good one." his daughter replied

I thought I understood what was meant. She did n't want to rest under an obligation, and so I was to be paid up for what I had done by promotion. It made me grit my teeth, and if I had n't taught myself not to swear, because of my position, I could have given sheriff Gunton points on cursing. I wanted to speak up right there and tell Miss Cullen what I thought of her.

Of the interview which took place inside 218, I can speak only at second-hand, and the world knows about as well as I how the contest was compromised by the K. & A. being turned over to the Missouri Western, the territory in Southern California being divided between the California Central and the Great Southern, and a traffic arrangement agreed upon that satisfied the G. S. That afternoon a Missouri Western board for the K. & A. was elected without opposition, and they in turn elected Mr. Cullen president of the K. & A.; so when my report of the holding-up went in, he had the pleasure of reading it. I closed it with a request for instructions, but I never received any, and that ended the matter. I turned over the letters to the special agent at Flagstaff, and I suppose his report is slumbering in sqme pigeon-hole in Washington, for I should have known of any attempt to bring the culprits to punishment. Mr. Cullen had taken a big risk, but came out of it with a great lot of money, for the Missouri Western bought all his holdings in the K. & A. and C. C. But the scare must have taught him a lesson, for ever since then he's been conservative, and talks about the foolishness of investors who try to get more than five per cent, or who think of anything but good railroad bonds.

As for myself, a month after these occurrences I was appointed superintendent of the Missouri Western, which by this deal had become one of the largest railroad systems in the world. It was a big step up for so young a man, and was of course pure favoritism, due to Mr. Cullen's influence. I didn't stay in the position long, for within two years I was offered the presidency of the Chicago & St. Paul, and I think that was won on merit. Whether or not, I hold the position still, and have made my road earn and pay dividends right through the panic.

All this is getting away ahead of events, however. The election delayed us so that we could n't couple on to No. 4 that afternoon, and consequently we had to lie that night at Ash Forks. I made the officers my excuse for keeping away from the Cullens, as I wished to avoid Madge. I did my best to be good company to the bluecoats, and had a first-class dinner for them on my car, but I was in a pretty glum mood, which even champagne could n't modify. Though all necessity of a guard ceased with the compromise, the cavalry remained till the next morning, and, after giving them a good breakfast, about six o'clock we shook hands, the bugle sounded, and off they rode. For the first time I understood how a fellow disappointed in love comes to enlist.

When I turned about to go into my car, I found Madge standing on the platform of 218 waving a handkerchief. I paid no attention to her, and started up my steps.

"Mr. Gordon," she said, — and when I looked at her I saw that she was flushing, — "what is the matter?"

I suppose most fellows would have found some excuse, but for the life of me I could n't. All I was able to say was, —

"I would rather not say, Miss Cullen."

"How unfair you are!" she cried. "You — without the slightest reason you suddenly go out of your way to ill-treat — insult me, and yet will not tell me the cause."

That made me angry. "Cause?" I cried. "As if you did n't know of a cause! What you don't know is that I overheard your conversation with Lord Ralles night before last."

"My conversation with Lord Ralles?" exclaimed Madge, in a bewildered way.

"Yes," I said bitterly, "keep up the acting. The practice is good, even if it deceives no one."

"I don't understand a word you are saying," she retorted, getting angry in turn. "You speak as if I had done wrong, — as if — I don't know what; and I have a right to know to what you allude."

"I don't see how I can be any clearer," I muttered. "I was under the station platform, hiding from the cowboys, while you and Lord Ralles were walking. I did n't want to be a listener, but I heard a good deal of what you said."

"But I did n't walk with Lord Ralles," she cried. "The only person I walked with was Captain Ackland."

That took me very much aback, for I had never questioned in my mind that it was n't Lord Ralles. Yet the moment she spoke, I realized how much alike the two brothers' voices were, and how easily the blurring of distance and planking might have misled me. For a moment I was speechless. Then I replied coldly, —

"It makes no difference with whom you were. What you said was the essential part."

"But how could you for an instant suppose that I could say what I did to Lord Ralles?" she demanded.

"I naturally thought he would be the one to whom you would appeal concerning my 'insulting' conduct."

Madge looked at me for a moment as if transfixed. Then she laughed, and cried,—

"Oh, you idiot!"

While I still looked at her in equal amazement, she went on, "I beg your pardon, but you are so ridiculous that I had to say it. Why, I was n't talking about you, but about Lord Ralles."

"Lord Ralles!" I cried.

"Yes."

"I don't understand," I exclaimed.

"Why, Lord Ralles has been — has been — oh, he 's threatened that if I would n't — that —"

"You mean he —?" I began, and then stopped, for I could n't believe my ears.

"Oh," she burst out, "of course you could n't understand, and you probably de-

spise me already, but if you knew how I
scorn myself, Mr. Gordon, and what I have
endured from that man, you would only
pity me."

Light broke on me suddenly. "Do you
mean, Miss Cullen," I cried hotly, "that
he's been cad enough to force his attentions
upon you by threats?"

"Yes. First he made me endure him
because he was going to help us, and from
the moment the robbery was done, he has
been threatening to tell. Oh, how I have
suffered!"

Then I said a very silly thing. "Miss
Cullen," I groaned, "I'd give anything if I
were only your brother." For the moment
I really meant it.

"I haven't dared to tell any of them,"
she explained, "because I knew they would
resent it and make Lord Ralles angry, and
then he would tell, and so ruin papa. It
seemed such a little thing to bear for his
sake, but, oh, it's been — I suppose you
despise me!"

"I never dreamed of despising you," I said. "I only thought, of course — seeing what I did — and — that you were fond — No — that is — I mean — well — The beast!" I could n't help exclaiming.

"Oh," said Madge, blushing, and stammering breathlessly, "you must n't think — there was really — you happened to — usually I managed to keep with papa or my brothers, or else run away, as I did when he interrupted my letter-writing, — when you thought we had — but it was nothing of the — I kept away just — but the night of the robbery I forgot, and on the trail his mule blocked the path. He never — there really was n't — you saved me the only times he — he — that he was really rude; and I am so grateful for it, Mr. Gordon."

I was n't in a mood to enjoy even Miss Cullen's gratitude. Without stopping for words, I dashed into 218, and, going straight to Albert Cullen, I shook him out of a sound sleep, and before he could well understand me I was alternately swearing at him and raging at Lord Ralles. Finally he got the truth through his head, and it was nuts to me, even in my rage, to see how his English drawl disappeared, and how quick he could be when he really became excited.

I left him hurrying into his clothes, and went to my car, for I did n't dare to see the exodus of Lord Ralles, through fear that I could n't behave myself. Albert came into 97 in a few moments to say that the English-men were going to the hotel as soon as dressed, the captain having elected to stay by his brother.

" I would n't have believed it of Ralles. I feel jolly cut up, you know," he drawled.

I had been so enraged over Lord Ralles that I had n't stopped to reckon in what position I stood myself towards Miss Cullen, but I did n't have to do much thinking to know that I had behaved about as badly as was possible for me. And the worst of it was that she could not know that right through the whole I had never quite been able to think badly of her. I went out on the platform of the station, and was lucky enough to find her there alone.

"Miss Cullen," I said, "I've been ungentlemanly and suspicious, and I'm about as ashamed of myself as a man can be and not jump into the Grand Cañon. I've not come to you to ask your forgiveness, for I can't forgive myself, much less expect it of you. But I want you to know how I feel, and if there's any reparation, apology, anything, that you'd like, I'll—"

Madge interrupted my speech there by holding out her hand.

"You don't suppose," she said, "that, after all you have done for us, I could be angry over what was merely a mistake?"

That's what I call a trump of a girl, worth loving for a lifetime.

Well, we coupled on to No. 2 that morning and started East, this time Mr. Cullen's car being the "ender." All on 218 were wildly jubilant, as was natural, but I kept growing bluer and bluer. I took a farewell dinner on their car the night we were due in Albuquerque, and afterwards Miss Cullen and I went out and sat on the back platform.

"I 've had enough adventures to talk about for a year," Madge said, as we chatted the whole thing over, "and you can no longer brag that the K. & A. has never had a robbery, even if you did n't lose anything."

"I have lost something," I sighed sadly.

Madge looked at me quickly, started to speak, hesitated, and then said, "Oh, Mr. Gordon, if you only could know how badly I have felt about that, and how I appreciate the sacrifice."

I had only meant that I had lost my heart, and, for that matter, probably my head, for it would have been ungenerous even to hint to Miss Cullen that I had made any sacrifice of conscience for her sake, and I would as soon have asked her to pay for it in money as have told her.

"You must n't think —" I began.

"I have felt," she continued, "that your wish to serve us made you do something you never would have otherwise done, for — Well, you — any one can see how truthful and honest — and it has made me feel so badly that we — Oh, Mr. Gordon, no one has a right to do wrong in this world, for it brings such sadness and danger to innocent — And you have been so generous — "

I couldn't let this go on. "What I did," I told her, "was to fight fire with fire, and no one is responsible for it but myself."

"I should like to think that, but I can't," she said. "I know we all tried to do something dishonest, and while you did n't do any real wrong, yet I don't think you would have acted as you did except for our sake. And I'm afraid you may some day regret — "

"I sha'n't," I cried; "and, so far from meaning that I had lost my self-respect, I was alluding to quite another thing."

"Time?" she asked.

"No."

"What?"

"Something else you have stolen."

"I have n't," she denied.

"You have," I affirmed.

"You mean the novel?" she asked; "because I sent it in to 97 to-night."

"I don't mean the novel."

"I can't think of anything more but those pieces of petrified wood, and those you gave me," she said demurely. "I am sure that whatever else I have of yours you have given me without even my asking, and if you want it back you 've only got to say so."

"I suppose that would be my very best course," I groaned.

"I hate people who force a present on one," she continued, "and then, just as one begins to like it, want it back."

Before I could speak, she asked hurriedly, "How often do you come to Chicago?"

I took that to be a sort of command that I was to wait, and though longing to have it settled then and there, I braked myself up and answered her question. Now I see what a duffer I was — Madge told me afterwards that she asked only because she was so frightened and confused that she felt she must stop my speaking for a moment.

I did my best till I heard the whistle the locomotive gives as it runs into yard limits, and then rose. "Good-by, Miss Cullen," I said, properly enough, though no death-bed farewell was ever more gloomily spoken; and she responded, "Good-by, Mr. Gordon," with equal propriety.

I held her hand, hating to let her go, and the first thing I knew, I blurted out, " I wish I had the brass of Lord Ralles!"

" I don't " she laughed, " because, if you had, I should n't be willing to let you—"

And what she was going to say, and why she did n't say it, is the concern of no one but Mr. and Mrs. Richard Gordon.

THE END